GIGGLES

HOLLY KNIGHTLEY

GIGGLES

ISBN: 978-1-958761-69-4

For my father-in-law, Mike

CONTENTS

CHAPTER ONE

The Perfect Gift

"It's perfect," I said, nudging Barb, my hand smoothing back my wheat blond hair with excitement.

Barb looked up from the stack of old photographs she was rummaging through hoping to find postmortem photos. It's a weird thing to collect, I don't get it. I've seen a dead body before and it's nothing to take a snapshot of and display in a frame, but we all have our kinks. God knows I have mine.

"What is and for what?" Barb asked, putting the photos down, her tone hinting that she didn't find what she was looking for.

We were in this hole in the wall antique shop on the outskirts of Atlantic City, in the rougher part of the neighborhood, looking for something funky to decorate my tattoo shop. I'd just moved into a bigger space and despite my large collection of strange shit, the place felt a little naked.

I like naked on my women but not when it comes to the vibe you get when you walk into my shop. I want you to be excited. I want the place to have a palpable energy. I want you psyched out of your mind you're getting a tat by the Lady Killer Caz Graves or a piercing by Barb. Most of all, I don't want to hear you complaining you've been waiting. We're all waiting, whether it's for a sick tattoo or to die. So shut the hell up and enjoy yourself with my funky little tat shop with plenty of strangeness to keep you occupied while you're waiting.

Admittedly, I have a tendency to fall behind schedule. I'm chatty and I'm a perfectionist. I don't use those computer printouts for my tattoos like the modern chimps that have turned an artform into a mindless job. All Caz Graves tattoos are designed by me and inked by me. I'm a real f'n artist. Not knocking my tattoo brethren—well, not fully—but when the machines take over Terminator style, I'll be one of the few tattoo artists that will still be able to ink you up without it looking like a prison tattoo. All that said, decorating my tat shop like an oddities market adds to the experience and clients love it.

My old place had the perfect vibe, but it was time to move to a bigger and better place with a better location. I love Atlantic City but with casinos opening up in just about every state on the East Coast, AC hit hard times. I'm not the pack up and bail when it gets tough kind of guy, but my high-end clients don't want to walk through the ghetto in fear they're going to get mugged by a cokehead or harassed by a hooker. And my clients, celebrities or not, are typically not the kind of people most would mess with. So, if they're scared, that should tell you something, and it did. I don't need one of my clients to get punched in the face like with what happened to Steve Buscemi in New York City not that long ago.

They say there's no such thing as bad publicity. I don't care what *they* say. Johnny Depp getting mugged outside my tat shop would be bad for business. It was time to move shop before I lost clients. I love the water and have to be near it, so I moved a few shore towns over to Ocean City. Got myself a nice store front with an apartment on top. It cost all my savings, but Asbury Avenue is the place to be in Ocean City and my property value has already gone up and I've only been there for a month.

OC is a family town and a dry town. I needed this move for

the family and as any recovering alcoholic will tell you, you're always in recovery. OC being a dry town was a good thing and on top of that, the beach and boardwalk brought in the rich. Taylor Swift came in last week. Yeah, that's right Swifty fans. Apparently, she vacations at the Jersey Shore every year. I couldn't talk her into letting me ink her. She just looked around. Don't believe me? I have a picture hanging on the wall to prove it, along with other celebrities that came into the old shop.

This move was the best thing I ever did. I'd never been busier, and the new place had an organically better vibe with exposed brick on the back wall. I just needed stuff to decorate with now. What stuff, I don't know. When I saw it, I'd know it. My shop has an edgy eclectic vibe that Barb calls tattoo chic. I like that— tattoo chic. I had vintage dental chairs reupholstered for the client chairs and have vintage signs on the wall, strange paintings, and kitschy nicknacks. Think dark arcadia meets funky museum.

But most of all, I have clowns. So, when my eyes landed on this unusual clown amongst stacks of crap, my heart beat a little faster—a lot faster. I had never seen a clown like this before and I'd seen my fair share of clowns.

I picked it up to get a better look at it. It smelled of smoke and old people, but that was no biggie, I could just spray it with something. It was kinda like those old school dummy dolls ventriloquists use, but it didn't have a place for you to stick your hand in its back and make it talk; however, it did allow you to move its arms, which were too small for its body. The face, which I assumed was carved from wood and painted by some master artist to look as real as possible, was frozen with this creepy as hell smile. It had bright red lips that matched its hair. The smile was enough to make the hair on anyone's arms stand up. But not me. The Graves, all of us, are clown fanatics.

The strangest part about this clown that had me examining it like a curator at a fine arts museum was its legs. They were—well, not missing, but cut off. Not cut off in the sense the doll was damaged, but it looked to be made like that. I couldn't see any signs that the clown dummy had been tampered with. It was as if the clown was deliberately made without calves and feet—like the clown was an amputee. It had to be the coolest thing I ever saw. A real statement piece. It would look killer in the shop. But I couldn't be selfish with this find, this had to go to my son. It was the perfect birthday gift for Mason. I'd be father of the year after this.

I probably looked like some tattooed version of the Joker smiling ear to ear at this clown puppet. I was a regular Jared Leto without the face tattoos. I don't do face tattoos, but I do clowns. One look at me, and you can see I'm nuts over clowns. Like I said, fanatic. I have my arms and legs and every other part of my body I can reach covered with clown tats.

My arms are inked sleeves of clowns. They're a patchwork of iconic classic circus images and pop culture icons from Jack Nicholson's Joker, to the Joker from Batman the Animated Series voiced by the one and only Mark Hamill, to Krusty the Clown, to Pennywise, to Captain Spaulding, to Ronald McDonald, and just about any other clown you can think of. But not John Wayne Gacy. I don't glorify serial killers. My tats always render tons of compliments. If not compliments, stares. Which, to a guy like me, is a compliment.

Hell yeah, it takes skill for a right-handed man to tattoo his own right arm, but I'm that freaking good. I'm truly ambidextrous, owing to the fact I was juggling before I could walk. So, if I could see it, I put a clown on it. The most important clown is my father, who was a professional clown until his death. If you ask me or anyone in the biz, my father was the best clown. He's a real legend in the clowning world and to me. I inked him to my chest to keep him close to my heart.

Greg Graves, better known as Greg Giggles, keeled right over at some kid's birthday party and is personally responsible for producing the next generation of clown hating pussies. What a man. Damn, I miss him.

I was excited when my son told me he wanted a clown for his birthday. It's crazy how the apple doesn't fall far from the tree. My father would've been beaming at the thought of Mason following in his footsteps. I knew I was. I was so proud of my little man.

This clown would not only be Mason's birthday favorite, but it would also be a cherished gift he'd keep all his life. One day he'd tell his own son how he got it for his seventh birthday from his kickass dad.

Barb bumped my shoulder. I pinched my nose, smothering my sneeze. She always wore way too much perfume. Dior Poison in combination with the antique store's aroma of mold and cat piss was a toxic amalgamation. With my sneeze averted, I turned to her. "What do you think?" I asked, my wide grin hurting my face.

The septum piercing in Barb's nose twitched like she was some twisted pierced bunny from hell. Barb's my best friend. We were neighbors back in the old neighborhood and have been attached at the hip since we were about Mason's age. My father always thought I'd marry her one day. I guess I grew up thinking the same. That was until she cut her hair, dropped Barbie for Barb, and started dating girls.

I oddly preferred it this way. It was a relationship with a woman I couldn't screw up. Barb knew me, the real me. Barb's more than my piercer and more than a best friend, she's a sister. Barb's been there for everything. She'd seen me through my dad's unexpected death, my breakup with Lucy, and has always been the one constant in my life.

Barb was there that day when Lucy walked into my shop asking for a job. Realistically, I only need one piercer. Barb's a workaholic and piercings don't take that long. But one glance at Lucy DeMarco and my heart almost stopped. I seriously almost messed up the tat I was working on. Her crow black hair in contrast to her light blue eyes hypnotized me. Then I saw her clown tattoo on her right shoulder and knew it was fate. I hired her on the spot as Barb's assistant. By the end of the week, Lucy moved in with me, and by the following year, she was pregnant with Mason.

I learned my lesson with Lucy. I can't hire women I'm attracted to. Barb hired Lucy's replacement. Apparently, once you have an assistant, you can't go without, and Trisha is a lesbian from her friend's circle. So, there's no risk of another Mason James. Don't get me wrong, I love Mason and wouldn't give up my son for the world, but men like me who are immature, insecure manbabies should not reproduce.

Barb made a noise that was somewhere between a sigh and a hiss. "Please tell me you're not thinking of getting that. You have enough clowns and that one—that one's creeping me out."

Normally, I trusted Barb's opinion, but she's been off since she split with her girlfriend. Yeah, the clown was creepy, that's what made it so great. It was the definition of tattoo chic. It had that vintage vibe mingled with strangeness. It was perfect. Not that this clown was going in the shop, but Mason's room. Maybe even front and center on his bed as his new favorite toy.

For being a toy, the clown had a lifelike quality to it. Not in the Chucky kinda way, but in the entertaining way. When my father worked for Buchheim Circus, I loved watching the puppeteers. The ache for my father felt like a fresh wound. Childhood memories swelled in my heart, and I wanted to do my best to give Mason what my father had given me when I was his age.

I bit my knuckles, a thing I did when I got really excited.

Years ago, I tattooed 'R-E-L-A-X' to my knuckles as a reminder to chill the hell out. I read it now, collecting myself. I really was a manchild. "Mason's gonna love it."

"Don't want to burst your bubble Boss, but Mason doesn't strike me as the kind of kid that would want that."

I hated it when Barb called me *Boss* and she knew it. It made me feel like I forced her to go shopping with me if she wanted to keep her job. And I also hated it when she acted like Mason was a sissy.

My head snapped in her direction. "What's that supposed to mean?" I asked pensively. If she called Mason a sissy, I was going to fire her. It didn't matter that she's my best and only friend.

"I was thinking you should play it safe and go with a dinosaur."

"He asked for a clown," I said with finality.

She quirked an eyebrow. The little black spiked piercings that ran the length of her perfectly arched eyebrow looked like the spikes on a dragon's back. If you could pierce it, Barb had it pierced. If I'm being honest, Barb's a little jarring to look at. Me with the clown tattoos and Barb with her pierce-everything-look could normally clear a room of mundane people. Personally, I never went for piercings, on me at least. I'm not into pain, only pleasure. Except when it comes to tattoos, tattoos are different. But I do like a chick with piercings, just not as many as Barb. I like to know my girl's not some manmade reptile.

"How old is Mason turning again?" Barb asked, snapping me out of my dragon reverie.

"Seven."

"Yeah, go with the dinosaur Caz. You already messed up Christmas. Your dad-hood can't take another epic failure."

Barb was right about that. I'd gotten Mason a kitten for

Christmas. This cute little black kitten named Midnight. How was I supposed to know Mason was allergic to cats? He broke out in hives and the whole nine yards. But I knew my son, clowning is in his blood.

I narrowed my eyes at my soon to be ex-best friend. "He's a Graves. He plays with clowns, not stupid dinosaurs. And like I said, he asked for a clown. Father of the year here I come."

Barb shrugged. Man, was she a Debbie Downer.

I took the clown up to the counter where a tired old man sat on a chair. He was withered like the Crypt Keeper, that's for sure. His stringy dark hair was combed over his chrome dome like spider webs. His skin was that gray color you only see on really unhealthy people who are about to kick the bucket.

"Hey, how much for the clown?"

The man adjusted his glasses but remained seated. "Where did you get that?"

I was thrown off by his response. Where did he think I got it? I pointed to the back of the store. "In the bottom of a box amongst other crap," I said, hoping my verbiage would make him lower whatever number he was about to say.

"That box shouldn't have been brought out to the sales floor."

The man went to take the clown from me, but I wouldn't let him. I tightened my grip on it like the Jaws of Life. I guessed my negotiation skills offended the guy. Time to act hard. Act—I *am* hard. My eyes locked with old four-eyes. I wasn't giving him an inch. "How much for the clown?" I repeated.

"Giggles is not for sale."

My heart did a cartwheel. A freaking cartwheel to a springboard. I needed this clown more than ever. Giggles was my dad's clowning name. Greg Giggles, the master clown of laughs. Talk about being meant to be. I knew this clown was perfect for

Mason.

"Listen buddy, name your price. I'm not leaving without the clown," I said, my voice as firm as my grip.

It was times like this I wished I looked a little more intimidating. I wasn't the muscular biker type of tattoo guy. I was toned with a nice build, but thin, looking younger than my twenty-eight years. If anything, I looked like a punk. But to *Mr. Burns*, I should've looked like his worst nightmare.

Barb made a growling noise that coerced me to glance at her. She was tapping on her knuckles, her way of telling me to relax. I didn't care how pissed she got; I wasn't leaving without Giggles.

The old man sighed. Or was it a gasp? Either way, we both turned to stare at him. His eyes danced around the store like he was looking at someone or multiple someones. It was strange as all hell how his eyes darted around like a trapped ping-pong ball. In unison, Barb and I glanced behind us, looking for the customer that drew the old man's attention. There was no one there, we were the only ones in the store.

The man's hollow voice made me whip my head back in his direction. "Giggles is not to be played with."

My lips curved into a smile that I tried to suppress. The old man was done playing hardball. "You got it buddy. He's going in my tattoo shop on a shelf."

This got a grunt from Barb. I don't know what she wanted me to do, tell him it was for my son and start back at ground zero? Telling him what he wanted to hear and getting the hell out of there sounded like the better idea to me.

The man tightened his grip on Giggles and so did I. I suppose he took Barb's animal noises as evidence I was lying. I was so close to the man now as I leaned over the counter, I could smell the coffee on his breath. His dark eyes were moist and small behind the frame of his glasses, and I wondered how old he really was. For as withered as he appeared, he wasn't wrinkly. I inclined my chin to my tattooed arm. "I'm a clown junkie, I have to have it," I said.

"Giggles is not to be played with," he repeated.

"And he won't be. He's for display only."

I decided to ease up. Maybe this old man would be a little more pliable if I came off more professional. I pulled out my business card and handed it to him.

"Ink Me by Cazanova Graves. Killer tattoos by a lady killer," he read out loud in a monotone voice.

"That's me, Caz," I said, flashing him my full smile, also known as the panty dropper. I received no reaction from the old man. Not even a slight twitch of the mouth. I wasn't trying to drop this old guy's boxers, but my straight male clients usually laugh.

"Haha, it's a play on words. Casanova, *Caz*anova. Graves as in death. Get it? Casanova was a lady killer, as in getting with them."

"I don't laugh," the man stated plainly.

"I told him to just go with Caz Graves and drop the tag line," Barb said.

I shot her a glare. "I recall it the other way around."

She shrugged.

The nickname *Caz*anova was actually given to me by Barb, and she was super proud that I went by it. She was really in a mood today and starting to tick me off.

My attention was back on the old man. "Like the business card says, I own a tattoo parlor. This is exactly the kind of thing that my customers would love to see."

"It's haunted," the man deadpanned.

"Even better."

"And you promise you're not going to play with it? I can't let you take it in good conscience, if I know you're gonna play with it. No matter what the consequences."

Barb pursed her lips, the clashing of upper and lower hoop piercings giving off the allusion that her mouth was pierced shut.

"Listen man, I'm almost thirty, I don't play with toys. I'm gonna display it in my shop on a shelf where no one will touch it. It's just a novelty piece."

"I have your word?"

"Yes," I said in a way I hope dispelled all doubt.

"I can't sell it to you, but I can give it to you." He released Giggles to grab my arm. "I can't say more, but to say again, Giggles is not to be played with."

"Got it," I said, thinking this old man lost his marbles.

"He comes with an adoption certificate."

"Cool, it's like a clown Cabbage Patch Kid," Barb said.

From behind the counter, the old man pulled out a piece of paper that was rolled into a scroll, kept that way via a bright red rubber band. Free of the rubber band, he unrolled the piece of paper, placing it in front of me.

"Please read and sign," he said, crossing off what I could only assume was his name from the list of names already crossed off.

I took the pen lying on the counter and went to sign it.

"Read it," the old man cautioned.

I read it out loud to appease him. "Giggles: The boy who wanted to be a clown and could only laugh." He pointed at the names crossed off as if that meant something to me, but I complied. "Marcus Gable, Steve Fairfield, Samuel Lemanski, Peter McDermit." I signed my name under Peter McDermit, thinking I should have written Mason's name, oh well.

I guess in the old man's eyes, the adoption was official now. No sooner did I sign my name, did he relinquish the doll to me with a shove. The jerk, he didn't even take the time to rubber band the adoption certificate for me. But hey, what did I expect for free?

I took the hint and Barb and I made a beeline for the door. I wanted out of there before the guy changed his mind. Peter McDermit was clearly insane.

As we walked out, the old man shouted at me from the counter. "Don't play with it! You promised!"

"Boy is Atlantic City filled with weirdos," I whispered to Barb, turning back to see the old man's gaze fixed on me. He looked like he aged ten years since I left the counter. I gave him a wave.

His eyes looked like black holes as he mouthed his warning to me again, "Don't play with Giggles."

CHAPTER TWO
Father of the Year

I needed to give Barb a raise. She did an awesome job wrapping the clown for Mason's birthday party. She found a box for it and sticking to the clown theme, wrapped it in balloon wrapping paper. She hit it out of the park with a big red bow and ribbon.

Normally, I was the throw it in a bag with no tissue paper kind of guy, but Giggles was special and required special attention. I was hoping when Lucy saw it, she'd think my new girlfriend wrapped it. Not that I had one, but she didn't need to know that.

Since Lucy and I split up, it was bad date, after bad date, after bad date. Nowadays, I don't even look for a second date. I've become a double wrap it one-night stand bachelor and hate it.

I also hate it that Lucy left me for Wallace Steinbach and is still with him. I think what bothers me the most about Lucy being with Wally was that he couldn't be more different than me. It's like she went out of her way to find my complete opposite.

Wally's a psychiatrist, the kind that can write scripts and insists that everyone calls him doctor. I can't stand people like that. It's not because he has a title, he earned that, and good for him, but his need to let everyone know he was better than them got under my skin.

There was that, and he also hated clowns. The tattoo on Lucy's shoulder that had sealed the deal for me, she had removed for Wally. The nerve of this guy. I never asked Lucy to change for me and even if he didn't ask her to remove the tattoo, I hope I never made her feel like she had to change for me. She was perfect the way she was. I knew more than ever, confirmed by years of bad dates, that Lucy DeMarco was the only girl for me.

I still had high hopes of us getting back together. Back when we lived above my old shop in AC, she dreamed of owning a place in Ocean City. That was a reality now. She hadn't seen my new digs yet, but I knew when she did, she'd have to feel something, see it and know in her heart I got the place for her, for us, the three of us.

This weekend was my weekend to have Mason. Last weekend technically was but Wally took them on a Disney cruise, thus pushing my weekend back. Normally, I picked Mason up, but I was going to come up with an excuse for Lucy to drop him off so she could see my new place.

My hope was that when Lucy walked over the threshold to my new apartment, she'd see that I did everything I said I was going to do. I stopped drinking, I was trying to be a better father, and I got our dream place on the most desirable street in Ocean City.

If anyone deserved a second chance it was me. And I was praying Lucy saw it that way. Literally praying. It's true it had been nearly half a decade since Lucy and I had been together, but my love for her only grew. Somedays, I felt borderline obsessed with her. If only she'd give me that second chance, I'd be her everything.

Wally opened the door, looking over my tattoos with what could only be disgust. I got a sick satisfaction knowing he hated clowns, and I was covered with them. I returned the scrutinization starting with his parted black hair and his wardrobe that made it look like he robbed it off a substitute teacher.

"Casey," he said, over emphasizing my name.

No one called me Casey. My father was the only one and when he died, I officially retired the name, switching to Barb's Caz.

Every time Wally made the point to call me Casey with that smug expression, I wanted to down a bottle of vodka clean and neat. Not cut with soda or with ice—just the good stuff and use the empty bottle to cut a clown smile out of the fucking grimace he always wore.

I have an anger problem, but it only comes out when I drink. That's how Lucy ended up with Wally in the first place.

I'd had a problem for a while, it started before Lucy got pregnant with Mason. I knew I was drinking more and more but thought I had a handle on it. I was still in control, but I admit I started adding shots to my morning cup of coffee and that one cup of coffee turned into a pot of coffee. Then I needed the liquid courage to stop my hands from shaking and this vicious cycle took a hold of me. But still, I thought I had it under control.

My drinking extended into the afterhours as I had gotten in the habit of partying every night after work. Before Mason, Lucy would join me in the city bar hopping, sometimes with friends, sometimes just the two of us. With Mason a toddler, Lucy stayed home at night, and I went out without her. Without her there to watch me like the manbaby I was, I got plastered every night, not sure how I made it back to the apartment.

On this one particular night, I told Lucy I'd be home early and came back late. It wasn't anything out of the ordinary. That sort of thing happened a lot. When I'm with the boys, I lose track of time. From when I went out, till the time I made it home, Lucy had called me over a dozen times. Each call I pushed to voicemail. When I walked in, she let me have it. Mason had a high fever that spiked, forcing her to take him to the emergency room.

I was apologetic, making up some lame excuse which I'm sure is lamer than how I'm recalling it. Then she hit me below the belt. She called me a bad father. Before I knew what happened, I slapped her so hard across the face I sent her sailing into the wall behind her.

I remember staring at my hand for a long time before mustering the strength to look at her. When I finally did, we locked eyes. She had never looked at me like that before. Her eyes burned with an unyielding blue flame.

"I'm sorry," I told her, my heart pounding like an executioner's drum in my chest. I thought it was going to explode.

It was too late for *I'm sorry*. The irreversible damage was done. One smack flipped my entire life upside down. My hand tingles just thinking about it striking her—how hard I had to hit her to make my own hand shake.

Lucy had always been very private about her past and didn't like talking about it. She told me only what I needed to know. She grew up with an abusive father and things were bad, very bad until her mother remarried. Lucy told me, before we shared our first kiss, she would never be with a man who hit her. I promised on the spot, I never would.

There were no second chances with Lucy DeMarco. I like that about her. I like her confidence, her conviction to stand by her principles. It was what attracted me to her in the first place. That, and the fishnets she always wore under her Daisy Dukes, and the serendipitous clown tattoo on her shoulder that was now a thing of the past, like us.

Lucy made one request of me: never hit her, and I let her down. I broke her trust. Christ, I damn near broke her cheek bone and I broke my promise to her. The truth is, I never thought I would hit her. How could I? Lucy is my everything. Her and Mason are my world. I'd kill someone if they ever hurt them.

The hard truth, that I didn't see before that godless night, was that *I* was hurting them. Before the slap that ended it all, I had been hurting them with my drinking and my neglect. I was toxic to my own family and Lucy had every right to leave me. I'm glad she did. In fact, I'm proud of her. It had to be hard for her to pick up a toddler and leave how she did.

Lucy took Mason to Wally's that night and has been with him ever since. She had been seeing Wally in a professional capacity to have someone to talk to about yours truly. So, on all levels of cosmic karma, I pushed her into Wally's arms.

Barb thought Lucy must have been two-timing me before the slap. But she wasn't. Wally was a friend of a friend, so she trusted him. I'd never tell Wally this, but part of me is grateful he was there for her and my son. As much as I can't stand the snob, at least he has a steady job and a nice house. And I knew he didn't hit Lucy or Mason.

Hitting Lucy was a real eye opener for me. Only the second one I've ever had, with the first being my father's death. I promised Lucy, as she packed her bags, that I would never hit her again. That I wasn't myself, that I was drunk. I made her a new promise to never drink again. And I hadn't since that night.

The next day, I found an Alcoholics Anonymous meeting, got a sponsor, and stayed on track. Today, I'm approaching four years sober. That's right, I was on track to get my family back. I purchased our dream home and my son's dream birthday gift was in my hands.

I pushed past Wally, trying my best not to let him know calling me Casey bothered me.

"You're late," Lucy said, looking as pretty as ever in a daisy sundress.

Lucy would always be lovely, granted she looked very different from when we were a couple. Not only did she say goodbye to her clown tattoo, but she also no longer wore her facial piercings.

To the trained eye, you could still see evidence of the girl she used to be, see the little hole in her right nostril and eyebrow, see traces of the past I was a part of.

"What are you talking about?" I said, giving her my sideways grin. "The party didn't start until I got here."

Mason came running up to me, wrapping his arms around my waist. There is nothing like the love of a child. Only a little kid could love a screw up like me. But that was about to change. I felt it in my bones. The Graves family was getting back together.

I handed Mason his gift. "Hey little man, happy birthday."

"That's a big box," Lucy commented, her eyes scrutinizing it.

I beamed. "Got him just what he wanted."

"Good, glad to know it's not another kitten," Wally said, going to close the door just as Barb showed up with a gift box decked out in T-rex wrapping paper.

"Sorry I'm late," she panted.

"You're not late," Lucy said, winking at me. "The party just started."

My heart fluttered like a silly schoolboy. I knew it. She still felt something for me. I saw it flash in her eyes. It was only for a split second, but it was there. She still loved me.

"Dad, can I open my gift now?" Mason asked.

"Not until after cake," Lucy said in a stern voice that was more bark than bite.

"Please?" he asked again, looking to me.

Lucy gave me those ice-cold eyes, daring me to contradict her.

"Listen to your mother," I said, winking at her. I wished it could always be like this. Just the three of us. Me, Lucy, and Mason— no Wally. I felt so close to having it all. I said a silent prayer, praying for my family back, hoping God was listening this time.

* * *

I kept my eyes on my knuckles until Mason got to my present. The voices of the other parents and children washed out to a dull hum. I was laser focused. This was it, Mason held up my gift and smiled at me, his bright eyes twinkling as he shook the box.

"Open it," I said excitedly.

Mason tore through the wrapping paper and the box in a frenzy, pulling out the clown. It hung limp in his hands as he stared at its face.

"You like it, bud?" I asked, waiting to hear his approval.

"I don't like clowns," he said, putting Giggles back in the box.

I must've turned ten shades of red. I could feel a physical heat scorch my face like I just opened an oven and jammed my head into the flames. Barb placed a hand on my arm. I knew it was meant to comfort me, but it didn't help. It set me off. I did my best to keep my cool in the face of the truckload of snot nose brats' parents who were looking at me like I just pissed my pants.

"You told me on the phone you wanted a clown for your birthday."

He glanced at Giggles, scowling as if I had just given him a severed head. "No, I didn't."

"Yes, you did," I said, trying to sound upbeat. I went over to Mason, scooting between kids to show him the slot in the clown's back where his hand went. "Try it."

Mason put his hand in Giggles's back, making the clown wave.

"See, isn't it cool?!"

None of the kids were impressed. One little girl actually started crying, but I didn't care about them. I only cared about what Mason thought.

"It's great Dad, thanks," he said, tossing Giggles back in the box.

"Open mine next," Barb said, pushing her gift forward. "It's from me and your dad."

Lucy pulled me aside, taking me into the kitchen. We could still see Mason through the sliding glass doors. He had Barb's gift opened. It was a T-rex. He pushed a button, and it roared and so did his laughter. I felt like I was in *The Twilight Zone.*

"Caz, what the hell is wrong with you? Where did you get that thing?!"

"Some antique store. I thought he said he wanted a—"

She cut me off. "You're an idiot. He told you he wanted crowns. As in crayons. He's really getting into his art. He's following in your footsteps."

As if he materialized from the ether, Wally appeared out of nowhere with Mason's birthday gift from me in his hands. "I'm glad it's the only thing Mason got from Casey."

"What's your fucking problem Wally?!"

"You are, *Casey.* You know Mason doesn't like clowns. I want you to take this thing with you," he said, placing the box with Giggles in it on the kitchen island and pushing it toward me.

"Mason does like clowns. He's a Graves. You're brainwashing him with your psychiatrist mumbo jumbo and Lucy too." I pointed at him, wanting to throw a fist. "I'm on to you. *You* don't like clowns and you're putting your fears in my son's head. You have no right to do that. He's not your son, he's mine!"

He chuckled, this smug chortle of a laugh. "Start acting like his father then. I knew you'd messed this up, so I already got Mason crowns," he said, gesturing to the Crayola Ultimate Crayon Bucket with 200 crayons in it on the kitchen desk. I had never seen so many crayons in my life.

My blood boiled. For a moment, I thought I was

spontaneously combusting right there in Wally's kitchen. How could I let this twat of a man show me up?!

I turned my anger on Lucy. "What's wrong with you Lucy?! You can't let this guy fuck with Mason's head."

"Don't talk to my fiancé like that."

I deflated like a hot air balloon struck by lightning. "Fiancé?"

"You didn't tell him?" Wally asked Lucy, shocked, his eyebrows reaching his hairline.

"Fiancé," I repeated, my entire body spasming. I was crashing now.

Lucy held up her hand to show me the ring. "Wally proposed to me on the cruise, and I said yes."

Wally put his arm around Lucy's shoulder as if to make his claim on her that much more assertive—like some fucking caveman claiming his woman. I glanced to Lucy, then back to Wally, to Mason outside playing with the dinosaur from Barb with his friends. I felt so alone, so isolated. It was as if I was having an out of body experience. I felt like I was dead, watching everyone live on happily without me.

"Caz," Lucy said, "are you okay?"

"I thought he said clowns," I told her defeated.

"It's an honest mistake. Crowns sounds like clowns. Mason talks so fast when he gets excited."

"Time to take the kid gloves off," Wally said, upgrading from a substitute teacher to a school principal. "It wasn't an honest mistake. You blame me for brainwashing Mason, but if you took the time to listen to your son, you would've known he wanted crayons for his birthday. You may be Mason's father Casey, but you're not his dad, I am."

Ding, ding. Wally: one, Caz: zero. I wished I would've combusted at this point. Wally was right. How did I mess this up?

Crowns—to make art. That made sense. Mason had been talking about art class on the phone and then he jumped to his birthday. I guess I heard what I wanted to hear. Was stick-in-the-mud Wallace Steinbach really better for Mason than his own father? What was the point in all of this? Why was I here? Lucy and Mason had already found my replacement and together, without me, the three of them would be a family.

Barb walked in. "Everything cool?" she asked.

Barb, my one constant, my only friend. "You were right Barb, I should've gone with the dinosaur."

"No," Wally, corrected, "you should have been the one to buy the crowns."

My hand tightened into a fist, my eyes seeing 'relax' tattooed to my knuckles. He wasn't worth it. The pansy would call the cops and press charges. And the worst part was he was right. I should've been the one to get the bucket of crayons.

"I'm leaving," I said to Lucy. "I'll be here to pick Mason up tomorrow night." There was no point in having Lucy drop him off now. My hopes of a happy family were destroyed.

"Don't forget the clown," Wally said, with an obnoxious push that almost sent Giggles sailing over the kitchen island.

Barb grabbed Giggles and followed me out the door. She said nothing as we walked to my SUV. I was grateful for her silence and more so for her company. I leaned against my Ford Expedition. The black paint was hot, the discomfort welcomed. I took out my juggling balls. I always carried them with me. When I got really anxious and wanted a drink so badly it physically hurt, I juggled. It kept my hands, eyes, and mind busy. It brought me back to a simpler time when I was a kid.

Barb put Giggles in the backseat of the Expedition before leaning next to me to watch me juggle. She liked to watch me juggle, always had. She marveled at it, like it was magic.

"Hey, you're really good at that," a teenager yelled from the sidewalk.

"Thanks," I said, not breaking my concentration. I was good at juggling balls, but not life. My father had been a great dad, the very best, and I was the world's worst father. If I couldn't put the effort into getting Mason a pack of stupid crayons for his birthday, I didn't deserve Lucy and I didn't deserve to be Mason's dad. I guess it was a good thing he had two fathers: Caz Graves, ultimate screw up, and Wallace Steinbach, father of the year and clown hater.

I juggled faster.

CHAPTER THREE
My Weekend

Lucy opened the door a crack, homing in on me with one blue bloodshot eye. "What are you doing here?" she seethed.

The indignation of this woman. "What am I doing here?! It's my weekend with Mason. With your little pleasure cruise last week my weekend got bumped. I guess you didn't remember amongst all your wedding preparations."

"Did you listen to your messages?" she asked, still speaking to me through the crack in the door.

My phone was off since yesterday and I gave it to Barb. I didn't want to risk calling Lucy and going off. "No, I didn't. Why, what's up? Why are you acting funny? Where's Mason?"

"Mason's not spending the weekend with you."

"The hell he's not," I said, my anger lacing my tone.

Mason only spent one weekend a month with me, and I worked my entire schedule around it. Normally, I worked on the weekends but when I had Mason, I cleared my schedule to spend quality time with my little man.

Yesterday, after I pulled myself together, I went out and bought every single pack of crayons Walmart sold, and I didn't stop there. I got colored pencils and pastels, and markers and art pads. I was going to make it up to Mason. Lucy was a lost cause; she was Wally the caveman's now. But Mason, I still had a chance to be a good father to him and I was going to be—like my dad was for me.

"Let me handle this," Wally said, from the other side of the door.

"I'm handling it," Lucy told him, turning her head so all I could see through the crack in the door was her dark hair.

I shook my head and gnashed my teeth. They were treating me like some freaking pedophile who invited *their* son to a sleep over. Mason's *my s*on.

"Caz," Lucy said, opening the front door enough so that I could see her entire face. "Mason doesn't want to spend the weekend at your place."

I huffed. "Why's that?!" I knew why. It was Wally. I was seconds from pushing open the door and grabbing my son.

"He's scared."

I quirked an eyebrow. "Scared?"

"Scared," she said in a hushed whisper, "scared of the clown."

"Of the clown," I parroted.

"He had a really bad nightmare last night. I had to spend the night with him to settle him down. He's never had one that bad before. He woke up screaming."

I could feel my face grow stoney. "The clown isn't in the apartment. It's in the shop with all the other clowns."

Wally said something. I couldn't make it out.

"What do you want me to do?" Lucy asked him.

"Tell him to leave," Wally hissed.

My jaw set. I *heard* that. I looked down at my hands and read my knuckles. Lucy wouldn't stop me from seeing Mason. I knew she wouldn't. I just had to keep my cool and not give her a reason not to let me see him.

"I don't know what to do Caz, Mason doesn't want to go," she said sympathetically.

"Can I talk to him?"

Wally sighed, this obnoxious exaggeration of a sigh.

"Of course you can," Lucy said, letting me enter.

I knocked on Mason's open bedroom door. He was sitting at his desk drawing. I had never felt further from him. Instead of running to put his arms around me, like he normally did, he bowed his head. He looked so much like I did when I was his age, but he had his mother's dark hair.

"Hey," I said, crouching by the side of his desk to make us the same height. "If you don't want to come over you don't have to, but I want the decision to be yours."

"I don't want you to be mad," Mason said, his cheeks flushed like he was about to cry.

I wrapped my arm around his shoulders. "I won't be mad."

"I'm sorry I didn't like the clown."

"I'm not mad about that. If you decide you still want to come over, you don't have to worry about seeing it. It's in the tattoo parlor with the rest of your crazy dad's clown collection. And remember, anytime you feel scared by a clown think of your grandfather. He was a clown, and I was almost one too. Clowns are meant to make people laugh and feel good, you don't have to be scared of them."

He nodded, his dark tangles falling over his forehead.

"So, what do you say, do you want to come over?"

Mason pawed at tears. "You promise the clown's downstairs?" he asked.

My heart ached. I felt worse than yesterday, if that was even possible. Here I was making my son cry. I gave him nightmares and now he's crying. "I promise. No clowns. I thought we'd draw dinosaurs," I said, noticing the drawing of a T-rex on his desk.

I gave him a light nudge. "What do you say, hmm? You want to come keep your dad company and help him draw?"

"Okay."

I took his hand and led him into the hall, almost freaking out when I saw Wally waiting outside Mason's bedroom door. He'd been eavesdropping. This guy needed to learn boundaries and I wanted so badly to be the one to teach it to him. What did he think I was going to do, twist Mason's arm to make him come with me? I chuckled to myself. That's precisely along the lines of what he *was* thinking. I know he knew I hit Lucy. He'd never mentioned it. As her psychiatrist at the time, doctor-patient confidentiality prevented him from it, but he let me know in other ways. Right in front of me, Wally always made a point to scrupulously check Mason over for bruises after spending the weekend with me. I suppose he meant well. He didn't know I was a changed man. To people like him, people like me didn't change.

* * *

My head hit my pillow a happy man. Mason and I had a great night drawing dinosaurs. He screamed in delight when he saw the art supplies I got him. That kid's really a chip off the old block. He's one hell of an artist already. And his new room, he freaking loved it. Barb and I decorated it in dinosaurs. Entering Mason's room was like stepping into *Jurassic Park*.

Later, Barb came over with pizza and ice cream cake and we had a second birthday party for Mason. He was thrilled when I pulled out the cans of Silly String. It's this weird neon string that shoots from a pressurized can. I got a shit ton of them from the Dollar Tree, and we went crazy with it, shooting it all over the living room and at Barb. She was a good sport about it. My heart skipped a beat when Mason said it was the best birthday he ever had and mentioned Wally would never let him shoot Silly String in the house.

I closed my eyes, feeling like the best dad in the world. I may not be Greg Giggles, but I was on my way.

* * *

I woke up in the middle of the night like I was stranded in the Sahara Desert. Pizza always did that to me, made me need to guzzle down a gallon of water like a camel about to go cross country.

I made my way into the kitchen. Taking a glass out of the dishwasher, I filled it from the tap. I had just about relieved my water lust when I noticed Mason was sitting at the coffee table drawing. The lights were off. The only lights came from the blinds that illuminated the room in horizontal stripes.

I walked into the living room, "Hey little man, what are you doing up?" I asked.

Mason hid the drawing he'd been working on behind his back. "I couldn't sleep, so I made you a picture."

"That's a good way to burn off extra energy," I said, knowing I had done the same, "but you need to get back to bed. You can finish your picture tomorrow."

"Can I stay with you?"

"Yeah," I said, surprised he asked. Mason had never spent the night in my bed, not even when he was really little.

"Come on," I said, "let's go."

"I just need to sign my name, can I do it really quick?"

"Yeah, little man, go ahead."

He handed me the picture. I could barely see it in the dim light; how he could draw in it, boggles the mind. I slid the dimmer switch to 50%, just enough to see the picture without squinting like a bat caught in day light.

Mason had drawn me holding hands with the clown I had gotten him for his birthday. Like his dinosaurs, it was drawn expertly. He got the creepy smile perfect. There was not an iota of doubt he would one day surpass me artistically if he stuck with it, which made me proud as all hell.

"Thanks, I love it. You have real talent." I placed my empty glass in the sink and the picture on the fridge.

* * *

I woke up in the morning to find Mason not in my bed. Having slept well, I stretched, ready to start my day. I made my way into the kitchen to see Mason at the coffee table again. He was back to drawing dinosaurs.

"Morning killer, you want pancakes for breakfast?"

"Good morning, Dad," he said, flashing me a big smile that showed off his missing bottom tooth. "Can I help make them?"

"Of course you can."

He rushed into the kitchen, stopping in front of the refrigerator to stare at the drawing he made for me last night.

I tousled his hair. "You did a great job on it," I said, joining him for a moment to admire his art before I got breakfast going. I took a bowl out of the cupboard along with the instant pancake mix, turning around to see him still staring at his drawing. "Hey bud, ready to help?"

He looked at me and smiled. "Yeah Dad!"

* * *

I closed my eyes to the sound of the ocean rattling my brain. That was the only thing I disliked about the beach, the sound that travels home with you. Well, that, and the sand that always finds a way to get stuck between my butt cheeks. I read once that the ocean sounds that ring in your ears after a splash in the big blue wet thing has something to do with your equilibrium being thrown off.

Whatever the reason for the waves crashing inside my skull, I didn't like it. That, in combo with lying on my back, made me feel like I was a floating corpse. I punched my pillow in an attempt to fluff it. It was slightly more cloud-like now and I placed it against my headboard so I could recline in a sitting position. The noise was really getting to me tonight.

It was the one dark blight in a great day with my son: the boardwalk, funnel cake, beach, and the OC sandcastle competition, which we won for an octopus devouring the city of Atlantis, making it The Lost City of Atlantis, lost in its belly. It was a hell of a Saturday. Tomorrow it was back to reality. Mason went *home* in the morning, and I went back to being alone.

I had just closed my eyes when a strange noise pulled back my eyelids. That was not the ocean trapped in my head. There it was again. It was a strange dragging, scraping noise. It wasn't as piercing as nails on a chalkboard, but it was freaking irritating. "What the heck," I grumbled to myself, getting out of bed.

I entered the hall, ready to yell at Mason for being out of bed. My jaw dropped and my legs wobbled underneath me. My chest compressed as if I was being squeezed, a pain shooting in every direction as my heart thudded against my ribcage. The hall was dark, the light that filtered in through the living room blinds couldn't penetrate the darkness that lurked in the hallway. The only light came from the white clown face at the end of the hall. It gave off just enough illumination to let me see what was waiting for me. Giggles was propped up on his too-small hands and was walking toward me like a chimp. The dragging noise was the stumps of his legs on the hardwood floor. As he came forward, his smile took on a sinister appearance in the poor lighting, his creepy smile twisting and twisting until it became something darker. I sucked air, too shaken to scream.

That's when I saw Mason's dark tangles. They were just visible over Giggles's fiery red crop of clown-hair as Mason scooted on his knees down the hall behind Giggles making him walk. I sighed in relief feeling ridiculous, my hands falling to my knees for a moment while I collected myself. I'm not a sissy, far from it, but when I saw Giggles at the end of the hall, my body became an overcooked noodle.

"Mason, what are you doing?" My voice sounded like I just got back from a jog and was fighting to find my breath.

"Giggles wanted to play Dad."

My teeth came down hard on my bottom lip, almost breaking skin. Had I told Mason the clown's name was Giggles? I had to have. I must've said it in his room when I told him not to be scared of clowns because of his grandfather Greg Giggles.

My strength returned to me and so did my voice. Play time was over, time to be a dad. "Bud, it's the middle of the night and I told you you're not allowed in the shop without me. It's not safe. If you wanted the clown, I would've gotten it for you. You just had to ask."

There was a back staircase you could take to get to the tattoo parlor downstairs without going outside. It was locked, but I understood now I needed a lock Mason couldn't reach. Mason normally wasn't the kind of kid to break the rules. I guess he had more of me in him than Wally thought.

I came down the hallway, hovering over my son and the toy clown, asserting my dominance over the situation without getting tough. "Come on," I said, taking the clown from him, "let's get you to bed."

"But Dad, I want to play. I have to play," he wined, reaching for the clown.

"No, you have to go to bed. We have to be at your mother's early tomorrow. Lucky you, you're going to visit Wally's mom."

"I want to stay and play with Giggles!"

I was ecstatic to hear him say this. Mason was choosing me over Wally and to make things even better, he wanted to play with the clown I got him for his birthday. The clown Wally had made a big stink over. This was proof Wally was poisoning my son against me and I was going to talk to Lucy about it.

"Tell you what, you have to go to bed now, but tomorrow you can take Giggles home with you."

"He wants me to stay here with you."

My heart warmed. "Well Giggles," I said to the clown in my hands. "That's not the way the courts work. Take it up with them."

CHAPTER FOUR

Play Time

Monday mornings, after having Mason, always sucked. I'm not a morning person. In the absence of alcohol, it takes me half a pot of coffee before I can formulate a sentence. And this particular Monday had already gotten off to a bad start. The landline had been ringing for nearly ten minutes. Barb was getting as irritated with it as me. She kept making those animal noises she makes when she disapproves of something. I grunted back. It's my business, if she thought I was going to be the one to answer the phone, she's out of her mind.

"How about you have your lovely assistant pick up the phone?" I called to Barb in a sickly-sweet voice. It was a jab at her. Trisha hadn't shown up for work yet. I was on the fence when Barb wanted to hire Trisha, but Barb vouched for her dependability. I think Barb just had the hots for her. Sometimes I hate it when I'm right. That girl is always late.

Barb made a roaring noise that oddly sounded like a T-rex and picked up the phone. "Ink Me by *Caz*anova Graves, Barb speaking."

Barb looked in my direction, talking loudly to make sure I could hear her. "Oh hi, Lucy. —Yes, he's here. —Of course you can speak to him."

"Give me a minute," I said to Biker Mike, getting up and taking the cordless phone from Barb. "Hey Lucy, what's up?" I pulled the phone away from my ear, Lucy was yelling at the top of her lungs, and it was coming through like static.

"Hey, calm down. What's going on?! Is Mason okay?!"

My pulse surged, thinking something happened to Mason. Why else would she be yelling like that? I locked the cordless phone between the side of my face and shoulder as I scrambled to pull my cell phone from my jean pocket, hoping she texted me something I could understand. As a matter of principle, I keep my cell phone on silent while I work. I'd missed a dozen calls from Lucy, no texts. "Lucy, is Mason okay?!"

"What the hell is wrong with you?!" Lucy barked.

I sighed in relief and a little in frustration too. Mason was fine. This phone call was about me messing something up. "What did I do now?

"I can't believe you told our son that if he doesn't play with the clown it's going to kill him!"

"Ww—what?!" I spluttered. "I never said that!"

"Mason's petrified to put it down. He's been playing with it since you dropped him off yesterday."

I tried to keep my voice down; I could feel the weight of Biker Mike's and Barb's stare and the stare of whoever Barb was piercing. "Lucy, I swear on my father that I never said that. He wanted to play with it, and he wanted to take it home."

"Honestly Caz, you should just sign your rights away and let Wally officially adopt Mason."

My shock made me silent. I couldn't believe she'd say that to me. She knows how much I love my mini me.

"Caz, are you there?!"

"I'm on my way." Click. I hung up the phone and put it back on the charging dock.

"Everything okay?" Barb asked, lifting an eyebrow in an arch of spikes.

"What time is my first appointment tomorrow?"

"9 a.m."

"Can you be at work for 7:30 tomorrow?"

"Yep, sure thing," Barb said like it was no big deal. God, I love that woman.

I nodded my thanks. I knew she could read how thankful I was on my face because she replied with an animal noise that sounded like a purr, a sound she reserved for when she was being appreciated.

I walked back into my space. I was glad it was Biker Mike in the chair. We go way back. In fact, Biker Mike was my first client. He was coming to me when I was still doing tats out of Barb's dad's trailer with a pen.

"Hey Mike, can you be here tomorrow at eight in the morning? I gotta run out, there's a problem with my kid."

Biker Mike stood to shake my hand. His handshake, as always, was surprisingly gentle for a six-foot-five biker. "Kids come first. I'll be here tomorrow."

"Thanks Mike, your next tat's half off."

* * *

I was all nerves by the time I got to Wally's. I knocked, reading the message on my knuckles over and over again as I waited.

Lucy opened the door. Her face was cherry red.

"Where is he?" I asked.

"The couch."

She let me in.

Wally apparently took off today to take a front seat to another Caz Graves failure. He was glued to Lucy's side like a guard dog, his too tight T-shirt tucked into his khaki pants emphasizing the four-month pregnant look he's been rocking since I met him. I didn't address Wally. I walked right past him and into the living room. Mason was sitting on the couch with Giggles on his lap. He was moving Giggles's hands to make them clap. A shadow of the past tore through me. When my dad would perform, I was his sidekick—Clapping Casey. My job was to clap at the wrong time, to make kids laugh at my stupidity. At the end of the skit, I would get it right and clap with the kids and everyone would laugh.

I came around the back of the couch and took a seat next to my son. Mason was as red as his mother and was crying. They were silent tears that streamed down his flushed cheeks. "Hey," I said, putting my hand over the clown's hands to stop them from clapping, "what's going on?"

"I have to play with Giggles," Mason choked out.

"No, you don't," I said in a kind voice.

"We tried taking it away from him and he went nuts," Wally reported, sounding a lot like a school principal.

I turned to Wally with the most scathing look I could muster. "Shouldn't you stay away from that word in your profession, Dr. Steinbach? It sounds rather unprofessional."

He crossed his arms over his chest. Ding, ding. Wally: one, Caz: one.

Now that Wally shut his trap, my full attention was back on Mason. "I never said you had to play with the clown."

"I do," he said, the tears falling more freely now, his voice coming out raspy.

My stomach churned at the sight of my son in this much pain. "Mason, no you don't. I think it's time for you to put him down."

"Giggles said I have to, or he'll kill me."

"Giggles is just a toy," I said without judgment.

"No!" Mason screamed. "I have to play!" Giggles's

malformed hands clapped furiously.

It was time to switch tactics. The logical approach was not going to work here. Mason wasn't going to give up the puppet and as much as I hated to admit Wally was right, Giggles was not a good toy for Mason to have. I understood why Lucy called me. Wally didn't want to be the bad guy and take it away from him. I was there to take Giggles so Mason would hate me, and Wally could continue his reign as father of the year.

"Giggles," I said, looking the clown in its painted eyes, "how about I play with you instead of Mason?"

"Don't feed into his delusions," Wally said over my shoulder.

I ignored him.

Mason made eye contact with me for the first time since I sat on the couch. His blue eyes were a sea of tears. "Giggles said he'd rather play with you, but you have to promise to play with him."

"I promise. Now give me the puppet."

Mason let me take Giggles from him. As a sign of good faith, I stuck my hand in Giggles's back making him clap like Mason had done. I used my cartoony voice. The one I used when I was a kid. It sounds like I just sucked a helium filled balloon. "Caz, you're so much fun. I want to come live with you. Wally smells."

Free of my horrible birthday gift, Mason ran to his mother, wrapping his arms around her waist, and sobbed.

"Problem solved," I said, getting off the couch with Giggles still anchored to my hand.

My eyes locked on Lucy. "I'm going to go; I have an overbooked day."

"Hey bud," I said to Mason, his face hidden from me. "I'll give you a call after work."

Wally walked me out. "Caz, I want to officially adopt

Mason."

"No way," I said, not validating his request with so much as a glance.

"You don't have to answer now. Think about it. You'll save a ton on child support."

At that, I turned on my heels to face him, taking a step back into the house so he couldn't close the door on me. He took a step back. I closed the distance, speaking calmly although my hatred for Wally dripped from my voice in a melodious hiss. "Money without a family is just paper. Mason is *my* son Wally and if you ever suggest adopting him again, I will punch your teeth out. And when you're unconscious, I will tattoo a clown to your fucking forehead so every time you look in the mirror you'll think of me."

* * *

I took the steps to my apartment slowly, dragging my feet like an old man. Today was a very long day. I was mentally exhausted. By the time I made it back from Wally's, my next two clients were already waiting. Beach traffic this time of year is nuts. You have every local and shoobie dashing for the beach.

Trisha, the world's shittiest assistant, finally showed up, so that was something. She thought one of those girly coffees from Starbucks was enough to appease me. It wasn't. She had the audacity to have 'Best Boss' written on it in place of my name. She's a moron if she thinks a ten-dollar coffee can buy me. I almost fired her on the spot and would have, but I didn't have time for the splash bath that I knew would've followed.

Giggles the clown, the birthday gift that I thought would win me back my family, took his place on a shelf in the parlor where he will stay until I die, never to be played with. I made sure I told the little wooden fuck just that on the car ride back to Ocean City. He ruined my relationship with my son and his punishment was to collect dust.

I dialed Mason's cell phone as I made my way into my bedroom. When he didn't answer, I called Lucy. "Hey, how's Mason?"

"Sleeping," she said, sounding just as tired as I was. "He passed out right after you left. I don't think he slept last night."

"Okay, I'll call tomorrow," I said, hanging up before Lucy brought up Wally wanting to adopt Mason. I guess with them about to be husband and wife, Wally wanted to include Mason. That was nice, in a way, if it didn't hurt me so damn much.

I entered the bathroom and turned on the shower. It was a quick shower then off to bed. My head pounded like someone was driving nails into my skull. It had to be the worst headache I ever had. I just wanted this day to end. Besides, I had Biker Mike coming early in the morning. I could use a full night's rest.

I got into the shower and ran the lathered soap over my forearm, noticing little red specks. "Great," I muttered to myself, "the red line must've a pinhole." I couldn't imagine the day getting any worse. Replacing a line was no biggie, but at the moment, it served as a metaphor for my life, like I was slowly bleeding out.

The hot water helped ease the corded muscles in my back and shoulders but did little for the headache. I toweled off, took three Tylenol Migraines, and hit my pillow like a ton of bricks.

* * *

"Alright Boss, I'm taking off. Don't forget you have Biker Mike coming in at eight tomorrow. I'll be here bright and early to make sure your coffee's waiting on you."

I donned a pair of black nitrile gloves, pulling the wristband back to make it snap. "You don't want to stay and play?" I asked Barb.

"No, I want to go home. I'm tired and your shitty mood has put me in a mood."

I clapped my hands together, the pace quickening until I was giving Barb a round of applause.

"Okay Clapping Casey, that's enough of that," she hissed through her split tongue.

"Caz doesn't like it when you call him Casey," I told her with a shake of my head.

"Urgh, you're being creepy. Don't talk about yourself in third person."

Barb went into the breakroom to get her things. I followed her, standing in the doorway.

She put on her cross-body handbag, turning around to find me as a barricade.

"Move, before I move you," she deadpanned.

I smiled, my face distorting into a wide grin until it hurt. She couldn't budge me. Barb was hardly five foot tall. I towered over her and had to weigh double what she did.

"Caz, seriously, let me by."

"But I want to play."

"I said I'm going home. Play with one of your clowns."

A laugh escaped my lips that wasn't my own. It sounded like a bunch of piglets about to get slaughtered. It was a horrible giggle.

"Caz doesn't want to play with me, but I want to play with you," I told Barb as another giggle fought free.

"Fuck, you finally lost it," she muttered. Her gray eyes darted around the breakroom like she was looking for another way out. "Caz, move out of my way now or I quit and good luck finding someone that's going to put up with your mood swings you fucking psychopath!"

Another titter of squeals escaped my lips. "Caz isn't here right now, only Giggles." I pulled Barb's piercing gun from my back pocket. "Ready to laugh Barb?" I asked as I pushed her against the wall. Barb's face scrunched up in confusion. Before she could react,

I brought the piercing gun to her eye.

* * *

I shot up in bed panting. My trembling hands fought to push my sweaty hair off my forehead. "Oh hell," I said to myself. I rarely dreamed and when I did it was nothing like that.

I plopped back down on my pillow, my eyes staring at the white ceiling as I groped my end table for my cell phone. It was early, not even midnight. I dialed Barb. Barb's a night owl and an early bird. I had no idea when that girl slept.

It went to voicemail. "Barb's phone, leave a message. I'll get back to you if I feel like it."

"Hey Barb, give me a call when you get this. Had a freaking crazy nightmare." I laughed into the phone, relieved it was *my* laugh. "And yes, I'm calling you because I'm scared, so call me back."

I hung up. Being that I pay Barb's cell phone bill, just one of the perks of working for me, she's really good about picking up when I call. I decided to try her again. Voicemail. I pushed Redial. Voicemail. Redial. I couldn't remember saying goodbye to Barb before heading to the apartment. Did she say she was going somewhere? I racked my brain, but there was nothing. I was more mentally spent than I thought I was. I tried her again. Voicemail. "Barb, remember Clapping Casey? When's the last time you called me that? Shit, ten years ago or longer, right? In my dream you called me by my old clowning name, but I wasn't me. I was Giggles, that stupid clown I got Mason for his birthday."

CHAPTER FIVE

Jokes on Me

I made my way down the steps to the tattoo parlor like a drunk, clinging to the walls for support. After my nightmare last night, I couldn't get back to sleep. I'd doze off for a couple of minutes to hear that laugh and be up for an hour or two to only doze off again to hear the same high-pitched squeal. It was going to be black coffee this morning.

Entering the shop, I sniffed in. I didn't smell coffee, but I could smell Barb's perfume. "Barb," I yelled, "I need coffee! Tell me you're starting it right now?!" There was a knock at the door. I glanced down at my watch, 7:45, that would be Biker Mike. He was always early. "Barb, Mike's here, I need my coffee! Don't add sugar, I'm taking it black this morning!"

I turned the corner to go into the breakroom and stopped dead in my tracks. On the wall, written in red paint, read: Clapping Casey. "Barb!" I yelled. "What the fuck?! That's not funny!"

I entered the break room and stumbled back, almost falling over. I would've if it wasn't for the door jamb. I'm not sure how long it took my brain to catch up with my eyes, but when it did, I rushed to Barb who was lying on the breakroom floor in a puddle of her own blood. Blood—there was so much blood. It wasn't red paint on the wall; it was blood from Barb's wrists that had been sliced open.

"Barb," I said, my hands shaking as I held her to my chest, cradling her. "Oh God, no." I smoothed her blonde hair away from her face to see her eyelids had been pierced shut. "Please Barb, be okay. I put my hands over her wrists to try to stop the bleeding. I knew she was dead but did it anyway. Her blood wasn't drippy but gooey. She'd been dead for a while, her face blue like a bruise. My Barb was gone.

That's when I heard the laugh, the same laugh from my nightmare. My eyes darted around looking for the owner of the laugh. "Who's there?!" I shouted. Gently putting Barb down, I got to my feet. "I'm gonna kill you for this and I'm gonna make it hurt!" I grabbed a chair from the break table to use as a weapon. "Show yourself you son of a bitch!"

There it was again, that squealing giggle that made the hairs on the nape of my neck stand on end. I couldn't pinpoint where the laugh was coming from. It seemed to bounce off the walls. I left the breakroom, trying to ascertain where the bastard was hiding when I realized the laughter was following me. The laughter was in my head.

There was a hard knock on the front door. It was 8:00 a.m.

"Play with me Caz," sounded between my ears. "You promised to play with me. Barb was no fun, but I know you'll be."

In a horrible moment of self-clarity, I realized whose laugh I had been hearing. It was Giggles—the haunted clown I bought with the promise to never play with it. "Oh God, Mason," I said to myself as I dashed to the front door, scrambling to unlock it. I threw it open and collided with Biker Mike.

"Caz, what's going on? Where are you going?"

"Mason! I have to get Mason!" I yelled, crossing the street to my SUV. "Barb's dead!"

* * *

I banged on Wally's front door with both of my fists. "Open up, it's Caz!"

Wally came to the door. "Caz, what are you doing here? And so early, I thought you didn't do mornings." He looked me over. "Why are you covered in paint?"

I pushed him out of the way, his morning cup of coffee spilling down the front of him.

"What's going on?" Lucy asked me, coming from the kitchen.

"Where's Mason?!"

"His room, why?"

I rushed into Mason's room. My eyes and hands raked over him, making sure he was okay. He was still asleep.

"Dad?" he said, opening his eyes.

I scooped him up into my arms along with his blanket.

"Caz, what's going on?! What's gotten into you?" Lucy asked.

"I have to keep Mason safe."

"From whom?"

"The clown. It killed Barb."

Wally had a towel to his dress shirt. "Let me get this straight, the clown you named after your father killed Barb."

"I didn't name it. It came with a name," I seethed. I looked to Lucy; she'd believe me. "It killed Barb. I wasn't supposed to let anyone play with it. But Mason did and so did I, and now Barb is fucking dead!"

I darted to the front door.

"Where are you going?!" Lucy yelled after me. "Wally, you can't let him take Mason!"

"Casey, I'm calling the cops!" Wally shouted.

"Good idea, tell them Barb's dead."

* * *

Grabbing Mason with no plan was a stupid idea. Where was I going to go? All of my money was tied up in my shop. And like I said, I'm not the kind of man to cut and run. My life's a testament to that. I could've moved on, got a new girl and a new family, since mine didn't want me, but I toughed it out and will until I die.

I'm not going to run away from some fucking clown. I'm the king of clowns. I'm gonna kill it. It's just wood and the fluffy stuff dolls are made out of. I'm gonna piss on it, then burn it. Then, I'm gonna toss my head back and laugh because Caz Graves is going to get the last laugh.

By the time I made it back to Ocean City, the cops were already lined up on Asbury Ave. And somehow, Wally and Lucy beat me home. I suppose they figured I had nowhere else to go with Barb being dead. Damn, I'm predictable.

I was glad Biker Mike hung around, on his own accord or because he was waiting for the detective to arrive, I'm not sure, but I felt like the cops were being a hell of a lot nicer to me with him standing by my side like an unorthodox lawyer.

When the detective finally got there, we all moved up to the apartment, minus Biker Mike, he was cut loose. The crowd was blocking the street and there was no way I was going back into the tattoo parlor without a gas can and a pack of matches. I was pretty sure my neighbors weren't happy when I moved in and now, I was positive. Not even there for a season and I already had half of the police squad at my door. Wait until they hear about the killer clown.

I was on edge since I arrived back in Ocean City. When I heard Giggles in my head and darted out the door, I hadn't thought to check if he was still sitting on the shelf. He could be anywhere— killing tourists for all I knew.

I was willing to settle the score with Giggles right there and then, but I wasn't allowed in the tattoo parlor. It was an official crime scene, and they were still collecting evidence and whatever else they do when there's a murder. I described Giggles to several officers, asking them to check if Giggles was indeed still on his shelf. Trying to describe a creepy clown amongst a wall of creepy clowns to a layperson is next to impossible. No matter how descriptive I was, they all just shrugged and gave me 'there's-a-lot-of-clowns' or something like that. I was hoping the detective, at minimum, would confirm or deny Giggles's presence downstairs.

The head detective, a man that went by Millbrook, wasn't big on answering questions. I like the name, it made me think of Mel Brooks, but I *did not* like Detective Millbrook. He was a real dick. You could tell this guy thought he needed pants with three legs the way he threw his weight around like he was *The Man.* To add to his dislikeability, he walked ramrod straight like a telephone pole was shoved up his ass.

"Thanks," I said to the officer who handed me a change of clothing.

I hadn't realized I was covered in blood until I got into the apartment and everyone's eyes kept darting to my hands and midsection. I was allowed to wash my hands, but I had to wait for an evidence bag large enough to hold my outfit to arrive before I could change.

"Change here and put your clothing into this bag," Detective Millbrook ordered.

I got it, they didn't want me tampering with evidence. The evidence being my soiled clothes but freaking really?! Whatever, I didn't mind changing in front of a crowd, it was just like gym class way back when. Besides, Lucy was there, she could see what she was missing. I not only worked on improving myself mentally since our breakup but physically. I was as defined as a Greek statue these days and I hoped she noticed. I also hoped she noticed how totally awesome my new place was, not that I wanted to get her here this way. The whole thing was tainted, starting with that stupid diamond ring on her finger.

Of course, the only ones checking out my first ever strip show were the guys—Detective Millbrook and Wally.

"That's a lot of clowns," Detective Millbrook said, raking over me with his eyes like I was a juicy piece of steak. I tried to keep in mind he was looking at me with a detective's eye and not Dahmer's, but in the moment it seemed one and the same.

"Yeah, I like clowns."

A woman in a black suit entered my apartment with Giggles locked behind an evidence bag. She was of average height and build and had her blonde hair pulled back into a bun.

Detective Millbrook pointed at Giggles. "Even that clown?"

I put my head down; little strands of my hair fell into my eyes. I couldn't look at Giggles. My whole body tensed like I was in the vicinity of an apex predator, and there was nowhere to run or hide, besides under my wavy hair like a coward. I had planned on pissing on Giggles and setting him aflame to dance the Macarena over his ashes, but now I couldn't even look at his creepy grin. I couldn't face Barb's murderer. I shoved my hands in my jean pockets so no one could see they were trembling. "At first, yeah, I even liked that clown."

Detective Millbrook ignored my comment, standing to shake hands with the woman in the suit. "Perfect timing Dr. Moore. We were just about to start." He inclined his head in my direction. "Caz, this is Dr. Moore. She's an officer and a psychiatrist and she's here to evaluate you."

"I'm not crazy," I said through clenched teeth.

"No one said you are, Mr. Graves," Dr. Moore told me. She had a pleasant voice. It wasn't condescending like Wally's. I eased up a little, only a little. I didn't like that she walked into my apartment already knowing my name and who knows what else. Detective Three Legs hadn't mentioned it.

Dr. Moore took a seat across from me at the kitchen table, placing Giggles on the tabletop, off to the side so as not to obstruct her vision. I glanced at the clown, a shiver going down my spine. His face was pressed against the plastic bag like he was suffocating, and I hoped he was doing just that, but that unmovable grin of his let me know he had the upper hand.

"Please, continue," Dr. Moore said to her colleague.

He nodded before locking his eyes on me. "Let's start with the basics," Detective Millbrook said, poking Giggles. "Where did you buy this clown?"

"I got it at some antique shop. The old man told me it was haunted. He warned me not to play with it, but I just thought the guy was nuts."

From the couch, Wally let out a steamboat of hot air. Why Lucy and he were allowed to sit in on my statement and God damn psych evaluation was beyond me. "Fuck you Wally! How was I supposed to know he was telling the truth?!"

"I'm going to have to ask you to leave, if you can't remain quiet," Detective Millbrook said to Wally. I was starting to like him.

Flushed and looking like an overripe Jersey tomato, Wally stood. I guess mister smarty-pants doctor wasn't used to being reprimanded. "I was just going to check on my son," he said.

"My son!" I yelled after him.

"Only one weekend a month," he retorted, and I could hear the smugness in his voice.

Ding, ding. Wally: two, Caz: one. I wished I had 'fuck you' tattooed to my knuckles so when I knocked that smug look off Wally's face, the look I knew he was wearing at that very moment, it would be a double whammy.

Dr. Moore must have read my intentions in my body

language and shook her head. I dug my nails into the tops of my thighs. It was all I could do to stop myself from getting up and punching Wally in the face. Why couldn't Giggles kill that asshole?!

Detective Millbrook pulled out a small green notepad from his pants' pocket. "What antique store did you purchase Giggles the haunted clown from?" There was a hint of mockery to his words and tone. I was back to loathing him.

"Um, I don't know the name. It's on Baltic, across from Crown Chicken."

The detective shared a glance with the officer who had handed me my clothes. The officer, who was leaning on the couch opposite Lucy, perked up like a cat at the sound of a can opener.

I pointed at them. "What's that about?! What's going on?" I was no idiot; they knew the place I was talking about.

"Did you get the clown from Pete of Pete's Finds?" Detective Millbrook asked.

I pictured the strange old man with the comb over. Scouring the inner walls of my skull, I tried to recall the name the old man crossed off so I could sign Giggles's adoption paper. It could have been Pete, but then again, it could've been Sam. This was useless, I couldn't recall it. "I don't know the guy's name, but it's on this strange adoption certificate that came with the clown," I said, pulling out my cell. "I'll check Google Maps and tell you for sure if it's Pete's Finds."

"Genius, where's the adoption certificate?" Detective Millbrook asked mockingly.

Heat rushed to my cheeks. I really hated this guy. "It's in the kitchen."

Detective Millbrook and Dr. Moore followed me. I didn't think that was necessary, but I don't know, maybe they thought I was going to make a run for it. The front door is through the kitchen.

I went over to the drawer, where I dump all paper things that aren't trash. It's a depository of receipts for the business mostly. The adoption certificate was on top.

"Who drew this?" Dr. Moore asked, pointing to the picture Mason drew of me with Giggles that was hanging on the refrigerator door.

"Mason, my son," I said, realizing she hadn't met him. "He's a heck of an artist, just like his dad." I was proud of my little man, but that drawing was going in the drawer with the receipts as soon as the cops left.

"The same son you bought the clown for?" Dr. Moore asked.

"Yep, that would be him. I only have the one. That's Giggles and me," I said, not that the explanation was needed. It wasn't like we were looking at stick figures. It was self-explanatory. It was clearly a drawing of Giggles and me holding hands. All it was missing was a rainbow.

I scanned the adoption certificate before handing it to Detective Millbrook. "Peter McDermit," I said. "That's the guy who gave me the clown."

The detective read over it and handed it to Dr. Moore who took a long time reading it. So much so, that Detective Millbrook and I were left awkwardly staring at each other. He broke the silence. "Peter McDermit killed himself last Sunday."

"Last Sunday," I repeated, my face twisting like my tongue was a lemon. "That's when I got Giggles."

His notebook was back out. "What else did Peter McDermit say?"

"Just that he couldn't give Giggles to me if he knew I was going to play with it. To which I assured him that I wasn't. I signed the adoption paper, and I left. He seemed a little anxious, but that could've just been him. I had never been in there before."

"Is there anyone who can confirm the day and time you went

to Pete's Finds and spoke to Peter McDermit?"

"Barb."

He lifted his eyes from his notebook. "Anyone else?" he asked.

"No. There's no one else," I said with finality, because there wasn't. All I had was Barb.

"Who's Clapping Casey and why is that message written on the wall downstairs?"

I chewed on the inside of my cheek; things weren't looking good for me. Either a killer clown killed Peter McDermit and Barb, or I did. I had no way of proving when I was at the antique shop. Not so much as a receipt with a time stamp because the stupid clown was free to a good home.

My license said Caz Graves, but it wouldn't take long for Detective Millbrook to find out I changed my name from Casey to Caz. And sooner yet, if Wally called me Casey, which he was in the habit of always doing.

"I'm Casey—or was."

His eyes narrowed.

"I changed my name when I was fourteen."

"Why's that?"

"My father was the only one to ever call me Casey. I was always Caz and when he died, I didn't want anyone to call me it again. It was a way of honoring him. Only he could call me that. He was dead and so was my name."

I had made the decision to officially change my name the day my dad died because it was also the day my dream of becoming a clown died. There would never be a Clapping Casey to go along with Greg Giggles. There was only Caz, the scared fourteen-year-old who lost his father."

The detective mulled that over, tapping his pencil on his

notebook. "How did your father die?" he asked.

"Heart attack."

"Does Clapping Casey mean anything to you?"

I shook my head. Not even Lucy knew about Clapping Casey. Only the old neighborhood and my father's clowning friends knew me by that name and good luck getting any of them to talk to a cop.

Detective Millbrook closed his notebook and looked to Dr. Moore who was still reading the adoption certificate. Talk about thorough. At this point, she should be able to recite it from memory. "What do you think Dr. Moore, should we have him committed?"

My eyes bulged. This was it. They were putting me in a straitjacket. Before I could protest, Dr. Moore spoke up. "Mr. Graves is in possession of his faculties; he's merely communicating what he thinks happened," she stated matter-of-factly. "That doesn't make him mentally unstable."

I did my best to conceal the smile tugging on my lips. I liked her. I'm sure Wally, or any other shrink, would've locked me up and threw away the key. I could tell by Detective Millbrook's pursed lips he thought he had a closed case—the crazy clown man did it. Thank goodness for Dr. Moore.

I got it, I looked guilty as all hell covered in Barb's blood and my name was written in blood on the wall, like hey I did it, arrest me. But what is it that they say? If it seems too easy, it's wrong.

"Before I go, I'd like to speak to Mason, if that's alright?" Dr. Moore asked me, handing the adoption certificate back to Detective Millbrook who passed it off to an officer to bag as evidence.

"Yeah of course," I said, my eyes finding Lucy where she sat on the couch watching me in the kitchen. Lucy was always a hard read. I was unsure if she thought, like Detective Millbrook, I should be locked in a padded room or if she believed what I said about

Giggles. I just prayed she wouldn't keep Mason from me.

"Can I be there when you talk to him?" Lucy asked.

"Yes. I prefer for both parents to be there," Dr. Moore said, her line of vision falling on me.

I nodded.

Dr. Moore took Mason's drawing off the refrigerator and headed down the hall to where Wally was waiting.

Lucy updated Wally, letting him know that Dr. Moore wanted to talk with Mason as if she was getting his permission, which pissed me off.

"Dr. Steinbach," he said with a handshake, getting associated with one of his cohorts. "I'd like to sit in. I've been Mason's second dad since he was a toddler."

"That's up to the parents," Dr. Moore responded in a neutral tone.

I gave Wally a taste of his own medicine, returning his smug smirk. He seemed to cower. I liked holding power over the great and powerful Dr. Wallace Steinbach. Thank you, Dr. Moore. Ding, ding. Wally: two, Caz: two.

"I would like him there," Lucy said to me, her lips flattening out to a thin line as if she expected me to say no.

I would never deny her anything, not even Wally Steinbach. With a flourish of my hand, I gestured for Wally to enter Mason's bedroom before me. Anything for Lucy.

"Hi Mason," Dr. Moore said, crouching at the side of his desk where he was drawing dinosaurs. I recognized one as the T-rex Barb had gotten him for his birthday. "My name is Rachel. I'd like to talk to you about the clown you got for your birthday from your father."

Mason turned to see his mother, Wally, and me by the door.

"Your parents are here to make you feel more comfortable. There is no wrong answer to any of the questions I'm about to ask."

Mason nodded.

"I was told your toy clown talked to you."

Another nod.

"When did Giggles speak to you?"

A shrug.

"Can anyone else hear Giggles?"

He scrunched his eyebrows together until he looked like a sphinx cat. "I don't know," he said thoughtfully.

"Are you friends with Giggles?"

Mason shook his head. "No, he wants to hurt me, like Aunt Barb."

She showed Mason the drawing from the fridge. "In your drawing it looks like Giggles and your dad are friends. Why would he want to hurt you?"

"I didn't draw that," Mason told her.

"Yeah, you did," I said shocked.

Dr. Moore shook her head at me, so I zipped it.

"Mason, you didn't draw this picture of your father with Giggles?"

He shook his head. "I know my dad thinks I did, but I didn't. I don't like clowns. I don't like to draw them, not even for my dad."

Dr. Moore pointed to the bottom righthand corner of the picture. "This isn't your signature?" she asked.

Mason shook his head emphatically.

I leaned in to get a better look at it. It read: MG as in Mason Graves, but there was something off about it. Mason always spells out his full first and last name when signing his drawings. I taught him that. That way no one else can take credit for his art. I hadn't noticed the discrepancy until now and was confused by it but chalked it up to me wanting Mason to go to bed before he was finished with it.

"Thank you, Mason," Dr Moore said, standing to her full height.

I squeezed Mason's shoulder. "Good job, bud."

He nodded, before going back to his picture.

I closed Mason's bedroom door. "Dr. Moore, I'm telling you Mason drew that picture. He did it in the middle of the night, I saw him working on it."

"Sleepwalking," Wally said.

"You're kidding me?! Look at it, it's a masterpiece," I said, flicking the drawing Dr. Moore still held.

"Sleepwalking is a possibility," Dr. Moore confirmed. "There are documented cases of people driving while asleep and having no recollection of it when they wake up. In Mason's case, unless he has a history of sleepwalking, I think it's a high probability he suppressed the memory. After what happened to his Aunt Barb today, I wouldn't be surprised if he forgets all about Giggles."

"He has no history of sleepwalking," Lucy reported.

"I wouldn't worry about it too much," Dr. Moore said as we made our way down the hall. "Mason will most likely work things out on his own, in his own time. Keep a close eye on him and look out for any abnormal behavior. If things get worse, seek a grief counselor, but as you have good help at home, I think Mason will be just fine."

"You have to keep an extra, extra eye on Mason," I said pleadingly to Lucy, "Giggles."

"Is in evidence," Detective Millbrook said, with the bagged clown tucked under his arm.

My eyes fell to Giggles's humanoid smile for a split second before my line of vision jolted to Detective Millbrook.

"Stay in town Caz. I'm sure we'll be in touch very soon," he said.

Dr. Moore left with Detective Millbrook. Not long after, the rest of the officers cleared out. Lucy and Wally took Mason home, and I was left all alone. It felt like a cold winter day in the dead of summer. I looked at my knuckles, my eyes traveling down my slender fingers to my nail beds. There was still a hint of red there. I went to the kitchen sink, grabbed the sponge and scrubbed.

CHAPTER SIX
Memory Lane

I let Trisha and the rest of Barb's friend group know about her death via text but there was one individual I had to tell in person and that was Barb's dad.

I got out of the Expedition, my feet striking moist earth. I was in marshland territory. Christ, it had been years since I stepped into Atlantic Ways Mobile Homes. The old neighborhood looked the same. My eyes gravitated to my father's old trailer. There was a new family in there now. A kid's bike was dumped in the front yard. It wasn't chained or anything, no one messed with the kids in this neighborhood besides the kids who lived here and there was this unspoken law about stealing from each other in the park.

Barb's dad's trailer was directly across from my dad's. It was like a lonely man community. Half of the kids at Atlantic Ways didn't have a mom, and Barb, since the time she could speak, played mother to us all, even to her father.

I knocked on the door. Bobby Viscino opened it, blocking out the light from within the trailer. He was a bear of a man. Where Barb had gotten her petite figure, I could only guess was from her mother. He wrapped me in his hairy arms. His eyes were so bloodshot it made it look like the whites were made of blood and his breath smelled of Proper Twelve whiskey.

Bobby V, as everyone who ever met him called him, was always drunk, but this was different. Snot and tears poured out of his face like a science experiment gone wrong. He knew about Barb.

Instead of inviting me in, he shoveled me into the trailer with his one hand like I weighed nothing. Inside, he plopped down on his beat-up lounge chair, the very seat that used to serve as my client chair when I started inking.

Tattoos saved my life, and I owed that to Bobby V. He had done some time in the tank and had picked up the art of the prison tattoo and showed me, kind of. After my father died, I moved in with the Viscinos. Bobby V got money from the state, so he was happy. The state was happy because placing a fourteen-year-old was beyond challenging, and I was happy because I got to stay with Barb.

My journey to becoming a tattoo artist happened by accident. Bobby V had the occasional client stop by for a tattoo. On such an occasion, he was so drunk, he couldn't keep his head up and his eyes on the target—an arm. He told me to finish it. The arm in question belonged to Biker Mike. Biker Mike had met Bobby V in the slammer where he received his first literal prison tattoo and came to Bobby V after his stint in prison because he was cheap. Barb's dad, in fairness, wasn't horrible. If he stopped drinking, maybe he could be decent.

Bobby had told Biker Mike I was his apprentice, so Biker Mike agreed to let me finish his skull tat. Bobby V, like everyone in the park, knew I was artistic. By the time I was a mid-teen, my art was already spray painted on local buildings. It was true, most passersby thought my impromptu murals were commissions and not some punk kid defacing a building, but still, I had never done a tattoo before.

I was nervous, but Biker Mike was kind and told me to go on, so I did. Finding my groove and loving it, I didn't stop at the skull that night. I inked an entire graveyard scene that Biker Mike still has on his inner arm.

Biker Mike was so happy when I was done, he squeezed me in a hug that almost cracked my ribs. He spread the word and soon I was getting people knocking on the trailer door requesting me. Bobby V took a finder's fee of course, but I didn't mind. To this day, Biker Mike gets what I call neighborhood pricing as a thank you for letting me ink him that day.

The money was awesome for a teen. I spent a little on booze for Barb and me and the rest was invested in myself. But it wasn't enough money, so I got a job and when that wasn't enough, I got a second job, then a third. I'd take any hours from anywhere. No job was beneath me.

With my money, I purchased better equipment, which led to bigger commissions, which led to better equipment and so on. That's how it went and eventually I landed my first break and was hired at Lucky 7's in Atlantic City as a tattoo artist.

The owner and tattoo artist, Ray Evans, said I was a prodigy. That he'd never seen someone like me. Not just my natural ability but my creativity. How I seemed to know what worked when.

When it came time for Ray to retire to North Carolina, he sold me his business that came with an apartment on the top floor at a great price and just like that, I was a business owner. From there on, I kept hustling, and I took Barb with me.

"She loved you like a brother," Bobby V told me. Not bothering to refresh his glass, he guzzled the whiskey from the bottle like it was water. A good whiskey has an aroma. If you're a drinker, you know what I'm talking about. I could smell it from where I sat on a wooden kitchen stool. I licked my lips in longing. I wanted to join Bobby V and wash my feelings down. Hell, I wanted to drown in a tub of Proper Twelve, but that death was too good for the likes of me. Barb was dead and I was to blame. Sobriety seemed like the perfect punishment.

Barb's dad howled a blubbering sob. "I always thought you and my Barbie would get married someday and make me a granddaddy." Bobby V was the only one who didn't know Barb switched teams and the only one who still called her Barbie. "Your father, God rest his soul, and me both thought so. You couldn't have one of you without the other. You two were like a rash and an itch."

A smile pulled at the corner of my lips. The saying wasn't as cute as peas and carrots made famous by *Forrest Gump*, but coming from Bobby V, it was just as heartwarming. I was about to start down memory lane with Barb's father when I heard something. I looked behind me, thinking the barely audible hum was coming from an appliance. The sound grew louder, and I knew exactly what it was. It was the laugh I had heard in my nightmare and in the breakroom when I found Barb. It was Giggles's laugh.

Bobby V blew his nose into a dishcloth. "Barbie always said you'd be the one to take her out of the trailer park," he said, using the same dishcloth to dry his tears. "You did good Caz; you kept your promise to her."

The laughter exploded into a roar. I could scarcely hear Bobby V now. I glanced down at my knuckles. "Relax," I muttered to myself. "He's not here, there's no way. He's locked in evidence with all of the other killer clowns from Hell."

I let my paranoia get the best of me. What if Giggles wasn't in evidence. What if he killed Detective Millbrook? What if I led the killer clown to Barb's dad?

I shot up, knocking the stool over. "I have to go."

"Don't leave Caz," he said, pulling me into his arms for another hug. I was pressed against his chest. The smell of stale alcohol and old sweat was oddly comforting in that familiar kind of way. I wiggled my way out of his grip and jetted to the door. "I'll be by soon," I said as my parting goodbye before jogging to my SUV.

With one last glance at my father's old trailer, I was back on the road.

* * *

My mind was bouncing around from Barb to Bobby V, to my father, to strangely enough my mother. My father had been honest with me about my mother when I'd asked him about her, and I respected him for that. I was eight years old when he said, as plainly as he could, "Your mother is a stripper called Nina Night, and she doesn't want children."

At the time, I didn't truly understand what a stripper was and had just nodded. Sure, it hurt to know I wasn't wanted, but I had the best dad in the world, so it didn't matter, and I never brought her up again.

Fast forward a few years and I'm at the White Pony. Well, outside it. I was too young to go in even with a bribe. A bunch of the boys from Atlantic Ways made it a thing every Friday night to wait outside in the back, trying to get a glimpse of tits. Every once in a while, one of the strippers would take pity on us and flash us.

One Friday, we got there late and missed the girls going inside. We were about to leave when one stripper came out to smoke. When I saw her, my jaw dropped. I always thought I looked like my dad, that was until I saw Nina Night. We had the same light eyes, wheat-colored hair, sloping nose, and slender figure. I thought she must've recognized herself in me because she put out her cigarette and beckoned me with a twirl of her finger.

The boys I was with were hollering as I approached. I ignored them. I had laser focus. Face to face with my mother, her breath coated in alcohol and stale cigarettes, she whispered in my ear, "I'll give you a dollop of a good time for a few dollars." I stumbled back, trying to create as much distance between us as I could and just stared. She was disarmed, evidently put off by my reaction. I looked at Nina Night, really looked at her. It was one of those moments in my life that changed me. Meeting my mom for the first time the way I did cut a wound so deep I will always have a scar. After that, I never went with the boys back to the White Pony or to any strip club.

I heard Nina kicked the bucket a few years back. She fell asleep with a cigarette in her mouth and went up in a blaze of glory. Good riddance. I hated her, deeply hated her. She's to blame for my father's death.

After that night at the White Pony, from time to time, I'd notice this beat-up sedan pull up to the trailer. I had seen it before that night but hadn't given much thought to it when my dad went out to greet the driver. But when I saw the honey blonde hair, I put two and two together. Sure enough, Nina Night was the driver, and my father was giving her money.

I never asked him about it, but now I knew why he worked two jobs and clowned on the weekends and was still broke. It was for Nina. He was supporting her, her drinking problem, and who knew what else.

It was one of the last days before I moved in with Barb, when Nina came strolling up to the front door of my father's trailer and I was again face to face with my mother. She had to know, a blind person would have, but all she said was, "Is Greg home?"

"Greg's dead," I told her, and she bawled. I thought for a second, wait—she does care about my dad. My hatred for her thawed. Maybe I got her all wrong. I was about to tell her I was her son and that I would take care of her from now on when she said venomously, "That asshole owed me a twenty." My disappointment chilled my blood, solidifying my unyielding hate for her. I hated her for her coldness, for her selfishness, for her not caring my father, the best father in the world, was dead. I handed her a twenty from my wallet and never saw her again.

Tattoos saved me, the alcohol ruined me. Having my own shop at twenty-one got to my head. I had it all, my girl, my kid, and I threw it away. I worked so hard to be like my father and ended up just like my good for nothing mother. My mother worked my father into an early grave, and I sent Barb to one.

I took a deep breath, taking a detour. I knew it was stupid to drive past the antique shop, but I had to. If the cops pulled the street view, they'd see I went by. They say, murderers always return to the scene of the crime, but I couldn't help myself. I drove by slowly. There was yellow police tape tacked to the door. Besides that, it looked like the same shithole.

With nowhere else to go and not wanting to endanger anyone, not that I had someone to endanger, I decided to go home.

I came to the back staircase that led to my upstairs apartment to see Dr. Moore sitting on the steps with Giggles still sealed in an evidence bag. Just seeing a glimpse of his fiery-red hair made me want to crawl into a hole. "Hi Dr. Moore," I said, more than a little surprised.

"Please call me Rachel. I just make them call me Dr. Moore at the station to prove a woman is better than them."

I smiled. I really liked her. "Okay then, Rachel. It's not that I'm unhappy to see you again, but uh, why are you here?" I asked, making sure to keep my eyes on her and not the clown. I knew I should be watching that stupid puppet like a hawk, but I couldn't. Sweat beaded on my palms and in my hairline, I just couldn't bring myself to look at him.

"I believe you about Giggles. I believe he killed your friend. And I don't think Barb was his first victim."

CHAPTER SEVEN
Nighttime Play

Rachel sat on the couch while I made a pot of coffee. Finally, I was going to get my java. I inhaled through my nose, smelling the hazelnut blend. This was just what I needed to settle my nerves.

With the largest mug I owned, I joined Rachel on the couch, turning my body so I couldn't see Giggles where he laid face down on the coffee table. Rachel didn't want any coffee. That worked for me, I was going to drink the whole pot. "So, you believe me? About everything?" I asked. Even I had to admit my story was bonkers. I was having a hard time believing a shrink didn't.

Rachel locked eyes with me, they were intense green ones, like the kind you see in cats. I didn't turn away, I couldn't, her eyes had me glued in place. "I believe everything Caz. I'm not sure why or how Giggles kills, just that he does. He killed my father."

My eyes widened. "What?!"

She ran her hand over the fabric of the couch. "It's why I joined the force and why I became a psychiatrist. I could make a lot more money in the private sector, nevertheless I wanted to make sure what happened to my family didn't happen to anyone else's."

My sweaty palms were back, accompanied by a knot in my stomach that had twisted into a pretzel. "Tell me everything," I said.

"My father was working a case—Peter McDermit's actually. The McDermit family was murdered, and Peter said a toy clown did it. The murders were strange and brutal like Barb's. Just like in your situation, all signs pointed to Peter McDermit, but there was no evidence to charge him with the crime.

The McDermit case was my father's first case where he acted as head detective, and he was determined to solve it. He dug deeper and discovered that a few months before Peter McDermit's family was murdered, Steve Fairfield's family was also murdered, supposedly by a toy clown.

"Steve Fairfield—that's one of the names on Giggles's adoption certificate!" I pointed out, having recalled reading that name earlier when I dug it out for Detective Millbrook.

Rachel leaned toward me, speaking in a conspiratorial whisper. "All but one of the names crossed off the adoption certificate have claimed a clown murdered their family. My father used that as his starting point. The adoption certificate speaks of the boy who could only laugh. My father was looking into who that boy was in real life when he was murdered."

She shook her head in what appeared to be frustration, her bun staying firmly planted. "They ruled it a suicide. It wasn't. His colleagues said the pressure of the job got to him, that the case got to him. But I know it was the clown. He got too close to the truth, and it cost him his life. I knew there was only a matter of time before the clown resurfaced. I've been waiting to avenge my father's death and clear his name. I had no idea this whole time Peter McDermit had Giggles. When I graduated from the academy, I looked for it in evidence, but never found it. Giggles must have been returned to Peter McDermit when his case officially closed."

"Did Giggles kill everyone?" I asked, my shoulders and back aching with tension.

"Everyone but the person who brought the clown home."

My voice was barely a whisper. "Even children?" I asked.

"Even children. Peter McDermit had three kids under sixteen. Everyone who signed Giggles's adoption paper had kids and had bought the clown as a gift. The only name on the list that doesn't fit the profile is Marcus Gable. I couldn't confirm who he is or was and if he had a family. I searched the database, and nothing popped. I'm unsure how old Giggles is and was thinking Marcus's story could predate the database. It's the only thing I could come up with. The pattern of murders is too strong to think Marcus Gable's family didn't fall victim to Giggles."

I had to put my coffee down before I spilled it. No longer could I control the trembling in my hands. The shaking had started in my fingertips and now ran up my arms and down my spine. I shook like I had hypothermia. I got up and grabbed a sweatshirt hanging by the door. I wasn't cold, I just couldn't stand to look at my own arms and see the clowns tattooed to them.

I tarried by the front door, methodically raking my fingers through my hair, the tangles parting under the pressure. "We have to stop Giggles before he kills Mason and Lucy," I said deep in thought, my nerves making me ramble. "How does he do it? Does he come to life like Chucky? Can we burn him? I really want to burn him. Or we could rent a boat and drop him off in the middle of the ocean, mob style."

Rachel took Giggles out of the evidence bag. I turned away and bit my knuckles.

"Are you okay? I thought you wanted to try to burn it."

I faced Giggles as Rachel held the toy clown. My eyes danced over his cold stare and wicked grin for a few short seconds before I was forced to turn away again. I could feel my sugar dropping. I was going to pass out. I sat on the floor before I did.

Rachel rushed to my side, joining me on the floor. "What is

it?! Are you okay?" she asked, concern flashing in her green cat eyes.

She had Giggles with her. It was buried in her bosom, its strange small hands seemly wrapping around her waist while its stumps for legs rested on her lap.

"I worked so hard to be okay with it," I said in a shaky voice.

"Okay with what? What are you talking about?"

"Clowns," I said as if the word was a bad omen.

"I don't understand," she said, her eyebrows stitching together in confusion. "I thought you loved clowns?"

I brushed back my hair, keeping my eyes focused on Rachel's emerald orbs. "I did. I loved them because my dad was one. And I wanted to be one too. I lied to Detective Millbrook. Once upon a time, I was a clown wannabee called Clapping Casey. My dad had been a professional clown before I was born and had given up the limelight to raise me. Though he still did events on the weekends, like birthdays. When he had a clowning job, I always accompanied him as his sidekick. I wanted nothing more than to be a clown like my dad Greg Giggles."

"Then how did you end up a tattoo artist?"

I took a deep breath. The trembling had long since taken over my voice and I needed to regain control. "When I was fourteen my father and I were the entertainment for this little kid's birthday party. My father was in the middle of his skit, when he turned and looked at me. It was this strange look as if he wanted to say something but didn't. Yet in his eyes, there was a message, I just couldn't read it. The corners of his lips fell first, although his smile was still painted on. Then the rest of his face went slack, like he was melting. He crumbled to the ground and just like that he was dead.

"The kids at the party all screamed, hell the adults screamed. I turned over my father and saw his eyes with their lost message and his downturned grin that was still smiling, and I was terrified.

"This fear ate at me, stripping away everything I was. From that moment, I was scared of clowns. Freaking horrified of them. This new fear kept me from my father. I could never be a clown like him, I couldn't even look at one. I worked so hard, with the help of Barb, to overcome it as much as I could."

I glanced at my knuckles, reading my message to myself, before I continued. "I still can't go to the circus. I still can't look a flesh and blood clown in the face. Hell, some mornings, I can't look at my own tattoos. I inked them there one by one as a reminder to myself not to let fear rule my life and as a reminder of who I'm supposed to be when I'm ready. Each clown I tattooed on my skin was a steppingstone to becoming my old self again. To the clown I was born to be, but I'm fucking scared Rachel."

Rachel wrapped her arms around me, bringing Giggles too close for comfort. I couldn't believe I just aired all my dirty laundry to a woman I just met and had the power to throw me in that padded room I'd been trying to avoid since my father died.

I shook my head at myself. I had no idea what had gotten into me. I'd never told anyone that before, not even Lucy. Only Barb knew about my coulrophobia. Only Barb knew I was afraid of clowns. Only Barb knew I was a walking lie.

If I had to take a wild guess, I'd say I shared my secret with Rachel because she understood what it was like to lose a father and for that anger and fear to fuel something close to an obsession.

Rachel tightened her hug, compressing herself and Giggles to my chest as her hands massaged my back. The caresses became sensual, her fingers teasing under my shirt. This was a bad idea. A horrible idea. Rachel would just be another warm body, which was probably what she was looking for, but I didn't want to give Giggles more people to hurt. I didn't want her to end up like her father.

A hand ran up my arm, another traveling down my leg. I

have little self-control, if any, and was finding it very hard to resist her. She pushed herself away from me, letting Giggles's face strike the hardwood floor. In an instant her suit jacket was off. She undid her bun, letting golden ripples fall over her shoulders. She was looking at me with lusty eyes. I knew those eyes well; she meant business. She took off her camisole top, which might as well have been kryptonite. I'm defenseless against breasts.

"I have a tattoo I want to show you," she whispered to me, her lips teasing my earlobe.

"Seek and find, one of my favorite games," I said in a husky voice.

The teeny-tiny bit of self-control I had was lost. Partly because an erection in skinny jeans is one of the most painful things I've ever experienced. There's no doubt in my mind the creator of men's skinny jeans is a masochist. Like I said, I'm not into pain, only pleasure. I had no choice but to unzip my fly.

* * *

I really needed that. The escape to Pleasure Island where nothing else mattered but fucking pleasure. It was a quick jump from Dr. Moore to Rachel to bedmate and it was the right move. I was confident she was feeling what I was by the smile on her face. Target acquired and satisfied courtesy of *Cazanova* Graves.

The day's events threatened to creep back in. I wanted to keep my mind on Rachel and on sex. I shifted my head on my pillow to look at Rachel. Her satisfied grin lit up her face like fireworks. My eyes traveled over her naked form. You'd never know there was a bombshell of a body like that under her loose-fitting work suit.

My mouth had been on every inch of her tight little body, and yet I never saw a tattoo. Nothing—just smooth ink-free skin. Rachel didn't even have the random beauty mark. Naked, she was flawless. I'd love to be the one to corrupt her body with my art.

"So, where's that tattoo of yours? Or was that just a line to get me in bed? Because it worked," I said to Rachel, my finger running down her inner arm.

She climbed on top of me. I grinned. I was sure it rivaled the smile plastered on her face. This girl was an animal, but I was up for the challenge. She leaned down and kissed me hard. I love it when girls do that, treat me like a boy toy.

Rachel unglued herself from my lips. I wanted more, but she pressed my chest to the bed, stopping me from kissing her. "I thought you wanted to see my tattoo?" she asked in a playful voice.

"I do," I said, liking her aggressiveness. I stayed down, waiting. "Show me."

Seductively, her hands traveled up her thighs, past her perfect breasts to her face. She sucked on her thumb. I was rock hard again. This girl knew what she was doing. Her other thumb joined her mouth. She used them to flip down her bottom lip. Tattooed to her inner lip was the word 'Killer'.

A nervous energy compressed in my chest along with the weight of Rachel's body. I wasn't expecting that. I had done my fair share of inner lip tattoos. This one was fresh. I was surprised she could kiss me the way she was.

"That a, uh, cop thing?"

She shook her head, her hand covering her mouth like she was about to laugh.

"A Marine thing, then?"

"It's a killer thing," she said, her voice muffled by her hand.

I'll play. The professional doctor has a twisted side, I can dig that. "You kill a lot, do you?" I asked, trying to sound sexy.

"When I can. There's nothing like watching the light leave the eyes of my victims. You can actually see the twinkle burn out like a star in the sky blinking out of existence. It's invigorating."

My heart felt like it was in a vice. This chick was being dead serious.

"I regretted piercing Barb's eyes shut as soon as I did it," Rachel said, making a pouty face. "I missed her soul's exit."

I pushed Rachel off of me, jumping to my feet. "That's not funny!"

Rachel stood naked before me, her hand covering her mouth to smother her laugh. I knew the cadence of that laugh—the quick rise and fall of a squealy giggle that made you want to cover your ears and yell stop. It was the same laugh I heard in my nightmare and later on in my head. I scrambled to find my clothes. Finding only my shirt and boxer briefs, I hurriedly put them on. "What do you want from me?!"

Rachel twisted her neck to look at me from a different angle. Her movement seemed unnatural, like the joints in her body had fused together. Moments ago, I had found her beautiful, but now she repulsed me like she was an alien creature. "Funny you should ask me that. I was wondering the same thing. *What do I want from you?* At first, I wanted what I wanted from everyone who took me home and refused to play with me after they promised their child they would. I wanted to make you feel as alone as I did, but now . . . I'm not sure."

I swallowed hard, my Adam's apple bobbing in my neck. This could be a good thing. Making me feel alone equated to murdering my family like Giggles had done to Peter McDermit and every other poor son of a bitch that adopted him.

I tried to remain calm as my fate and the fate of my family were decided by a clown puppet. But how could I? I was looking and talking to Rachel, but she wasn't Rachel, she was Giggles. How long had Giggles been in the driver's seat? Had I spilled my darkest fears to my mortal enemy? Did I just have amazing sex with a girl possessed by a haunted clown—the same clown that killed Barb?!

How the hell was this happening?! Could Giggles possess anyone at any time?! I looked down at my knuckles, reading my message to myself before I hyperventilated. There had to be a method to the madness or there'd be a lot more death by clown reports to the Ocean City Police Department.

"Okay, let's talk," I said palms down, trying to defuse Giggles from doing whatever he was thinking of doing. "I'm willing to play or do whatever you want. Just don't hurt my family and Rachel."

The corners of Rachel's lips turned up as she fondled her breasts. Usually something like that would turn me on, but it had the opposite effect. I swallowed a mouthful of vomit, the bile burning the lining of my esophagus.

"I had planned on having you kill Rachel tonight. I thought that would be funny."

My body twitched like an electric current just passed through it. "Me, kill Rachel?!"

She nodded. "Yes you. Just like you killed Barb."

The jolt of shock continued. My entire body was in tremors. I rested my knees against my bed for support. "What are you talking about?" I asked, my chest heaving.

"I jumped into your body just like I jumped into Rachel's. Once you play with me you give me permission to jump inside you anytime I want. I've been popping in and out of Rachel all day. I've let her dictate her own actions but have popped in to say what I wanted." Again, Rachel turned down her bottom lip to let me read her tattoo. "I'm clever, I don't raise red flags. I can seamlessly move in and out of my playmates. I've had lots of practice."

My mind went to the strange nightmare I had of hurting Barb. Had that all really happened?

"I can jump into Mason, you, and Rachel. Rachel just couldn't resist playing with me as she tried to figure out how I murdered her father. Which I did. I used Peter McDermit to help me with that. No longer finding Peter interesting, it was time for him to die by his own hands. I usually always do it that way when someone new adopts me. Suicides usually get swept under the rug."

I stared at my hands, "I killed Barb."

Rachel closed the distance between us, taking my hands. I let her, there was no fight left in me. "Yes Caz, your hands killed Barb. And I want them to kill Rachel."

My eyes lifted to Rachel's. They looked the same as they had since I met her that morning, poignant green. "Please, don't make me. I'll do anything."

She squeezed my hands. "I waited so long to find a new home," Giggles told me in Rachel's voice. "When you picked me up at Peter's antique shop, I instantly disliked you. I was eager to teach you a lesson because you reminded me so much of my father."

I avoided Rachel's gaze. Like a scared child, I nibbled on my bottom lip. I wished for Barb. I wished for my father. I wished for anyone who ever gave a damn about me, to help me.

With her hand still holding mine, she lifted my chin so she could look into my eyes. "But Caz, you don't remind me of my father, you remind me of myself. I can't believe I didn't see it in you until tonight.

"My father was also a clown, but unlike your father he had no time for me. When he came home, all he would talk about is the circus and I wanted nothing more than to go with him. He never took me, not once. He hated me. I'm not sure why. Maybe it was because I reminded him of my mother who died in childbirth. Maybe it was because of my new mom as he remarried and together, they had their own child. Or maybe it was because he thought I would be a horrible clown. I couldn't juggle. I couldn't deliver a joke. All I could do was laugh. But I didn't let that stop me. You see, I had a magic book that showed me how to perform all sorts of wonderful tricks. I was good at it and learned quickly. I didn't have to tell jokes and juggle to work at the circus. I could perform magic tricks. My dream was to perform as Marcus the Magic Clown while my father performed alongside me."

"Marcus—you're Marcus Gable," I said. "The one person who didn't fit the pattern of murders."

Rachel tightened her grip on my hands. She was hurting me, but I didn't complain. "In life I was Marcus Gable, in death I'm Giggles. I never did become the clown I dreamed of being. My dream was cut short by my father.

"It was time for me to perform my first big act and I decided to go with the classic saw-a-person-in-half. I constructed the box for the illusion myself in the garage with scraps of wood and used one of my father's saw blades for the always menacing saw that would cut me in half.

"I needed an assistant to pull it off and my baby sister, who was younger than Mason is now, was perfect. She just had to untie the knot holding the blade above the box. We practiced the act a dozen times. Each time it worked perfectly. The moment was upon me. With my father and stepmother gathered in the garage and my sister in her Sunday dress, I climbed into the box. My part was simple. All I had to do was tuck my legs under myself to ensure when the blade came down it cut through air.

"I was in position, my legs tucked under me. I gave my sister the signal, which was a wink. My sister untied the blade, and it came down just as planned. What I hadn't planned for was my father. Seeing that I used a real blade, and knowing how the act went, he went to stop it. But it was too late, everything was set in motion.

"My father pushed the box I was in out of the way, shifting it over and changing the trajectory of the blade. Startled by my father's sudden response, I stretched my legs back into the box. When the saw blade came down it cut through my legs, and I ended up an amputee."

My pulse was racing, but the blood wasn't traveling to my extremities fast enough. For a second I wobbled. "I'm sorry that happened to you," I said, finding my footing and meaning every word of it.

Rachel's eyes flashed with emotion. "At first, it was the best thing that ever happened to me. Everyone was so nice and showered me with attention, no one more than my father. He blamed himself for his love of the circus and for interfering with my magic act. He even stopped hitting me. I thought it was because he loved me. But in time, I came to know it was pity. Shameful pity that mutated into a bitter resentment of me.

"Right after my accident, my father had a custom clown amputee puppet made for me. It could sit on my lap, and I could make it clap. He named the clown Giggles and told me laughing is the most important thing a clown could do. The gift touched me. Really touched me. Giggles was my way to still be a clown. My father promised me that Giggles and I could accompany him to the circus. Like you did for your dad, I would clap for him and laugh with him. That's what he'd told me at least. That I'd be a sidekick, but just like before, he never took me with him to the circus.

"I waited two long years after I lost my legs to join my father by his side. I was the same age you were when you lost your father, fourteen, when I finally got to see my father perform. My little sister and I were able to convince my stepmother to take us to the circus for my birthday and as a family we went to see my father.

"That day I couldn't find Giggles and was forced to leave the house without him so we could make it to the circus in time. As I rolled myself on the circus grounds, excited to finally be where I belonged, I heard my father's laugh. I turned my chair in the direction of his laugh. My little sister and stepmother raced to catch up with me as I zoomed on.

"The crowd parted for me, and I had a front row seat to my father's performance. He had Giggles and he was talking to him like he was me. "Giggles Gimp-legs can't you do anything right?" My father asked the clown.

The clown clapped in response.

"Giggles Gimp-legs can't juggle, isn't that right?"

The clown clapped and children laughed.

"Giggles Gimp-legs can't tell a joke, isn't that right?"

The clown clapped again, followed by more laughter.

"Giggles Gimp-legs is so silly, he cut his legs off, making him half his height!" he said, shaking one of Giggles's stumps in my direction. "Giggles Gimp-legs can't do anything right and now he's half his height and he still can't figure out he's not the one meant for the spotlight. It's me the head clown, with my face painted with a smile and not a frown, that's going to make you laugh tonight! Giggles Gimp-legs, isn't that right?"

"Giggles clapped and the crowd roared with laughter. Inside me something snapped. I knew now why my father named the clown he had made for me Giggles. I was the joke. At that very instant, I lost my father. The love I had for him morphed into burning hate. He was mocking my love for him to strangers. Mocking the loss of my legs, which I lost in my attempt to make him proud.

"That night my father beat me. He hadn't since I lost my legs, and he made up for it. But it was the last time. That night my house went up in flames."

I had thought Giggles smelled like smoke when I found him in the antique shop. "You died in that fire, didn't you?" I asked.

"I did. I woke up finding myself trapped inside the clown unable to move or speak. I was moved from place to place in that condition until something wonderful happened. A little girl played with me, and I found myself inside of her. I learned that I could move between my playmates at will. I liked her entire family but not her father. Just like I did with Mason, I had the little girl make her father play with me and then I used him to kill his entire family. I punished all of the fathers, the way mine should've been punished. I wanted them to know what it felt like to be alone."

I held my breath. It all made sense, why Mason told Lucy he had to play with the clown. Giggles used Mason to get to me, so he could jump inside my body and kill everyone I love. Giggles had been in the driver's seat when Mason retrieved the clown puppet from the tattoo parlor that night he slept over. It was Giggles who drew the picture of us holding hands. MG are the initials for Marcus Gable. And I was the one who made Mason stick his hand inside the clown and make him clap. I started it. I gave Giggles the power over my family. Barb was already dead, and I knew what was coming next.

I trembled again, the wave of anxiety making my knees knock together and my heart thrash against my ribcage. I didn't know how much longer I would be standing. I felt like at any minute my body would just give out. It looked like I was going to go the same way my father did—a heart attack.

Rachel held fast to my hands. They were no longer clammy but cold, ice cold. "You're different from the others Caz, you're like me," she said, her eyes riveted on my face. "We wanted the same things, to please our fathers and be clowns. Together, we could still do that. We could be a team. Clapping Casey and Giggles—just like it was supposed to be with your father. What do you say?"

The vein in my forehead pulsated, making my eye twitch. "In a perfect world that sounds great," I said, unsure how Giggles would take what I was about to tell him. "I'd like that more than anything, but you know that I can't. I wasn't kidding when I told Rachel I was afraid of clowns. I can't join the circus with you."

Rachel's face was somewhere between a smile and a frown before it became a menacing grimace. "Not yet," I said, my voice cracking. I was walking a thin line. "Maybe, one day, with your help, I *could* be a clown. Until then, there's no reason why we can't still be a team. You can come with me everywhere—to work and at night come back to the apartment. You can have the spare room next to Mason's. We can be a family. I did adopt you, so that makes me your father. You can come everywhere with me just like you wanted to do with your own dad."

I was back to holding my breath. This was it. Giggles was either going to become my shadow or use me to kill Rachel, Lucy, and Mason. According to Barb and Lucy, I could be very manipulative, so I prayed this personality flaw didn't fail me now. Giggles was killing out of the hatred he had for his father. The reason he hated him so much was because at first, he loved him. I offered Giggles what he really wanted. He was just a kid after all, a kid who wanted the love of a father. In a strange way, we were alike, but I was also a father and could give him something he never had. I just hoped Giggles saw it that way.

"Go with you everywhere?" Rachel asked. I had Giggles thinking about it, I could tell. Rachel's eyebrows were scrunched together in what could only be thought.

"Everywhere," I confirmed, my voice finding itself. "To the store. To work. The bathroom. Vacation. The beach. Everywhere. But there are ground rules to being attached to me. No body hopping and no killing. Make me that promise, and I will never exclude you. You will go with me everywhere, always."

"Promise?"

"I promise. Cross my heart and hope to die," I said with certainty.

"You've already proven to be a liar Caz. How can I trust you?"

"You have all the power," I pointed out. "If I lie, you can kill everyone. There's no better insurance policy than that."

"I think there is," she said, taking a step away from me and twirling around like a demented ballerina. I really wished she would put some clothes on. "This time around I'm choosing my family, and I want to make sure I get it right," she told me, her mouth in a rictus grin. "I want to know that you would do anything for me just like you would do for Mason and Lucy. Only then, will I keep my promise to you."

"That's fair, that makes sense," I said. "Actions speak louder than words. You want proof you're family, I respect that. How about I tattoo you to my body. You can't get more permanent than that?"

The corners of Rachel's lips twisted upward. "I had something else in mind. I was thinking we make a blood pact."

With furrowed eyebrows, I asked, "Blood pact?"

"We're not blood, but I want us to be. I want us to be blood brothers and to do that we have to kill together. It's the only way I'll keep my promise to you."

My blood felt like mud in my veins. "Kill?"

"Just one kill Caz, to prove you want this. Barb didn't count. It was your hands and my mind. You have to do the killing body and soul. I know you have it in you, you're just like me. Prove yourself to me and I will return to the clown where I will watch and listen but never hurt anyone again."

I pinched the bridge of my nose as a massive migraine shot through my skull. Giggles was right, I had it in me, but I wasn't going to tell him that.

"I want us to kill Rachel together. You do it while I watch in the clown."

"Rachel . . . but she's nice, really nice."

"It feels full circle for me. I killed her father, and I feel I should kill her. With you—together. In a sick way, she's been craving this her entire life. We'd be doing her a favor. But in the end, the choice is yours Caz."

My mind was whirling, a hurricane of ideas whipping around inside my skull. I had to stall for time. I had to save Rachel. "I have a better idea, to really make us blood brothers," I told Giggles. "You want me to kill with you, but I'd only be killing Rachel to save my family because I knew if I didn't, you'd kill Mason and Lucy. Let's kill Wally Steinbach instead. I'd enjoy it and I'm sure you'd enjoy watching it. Besides, things could get messy if we killed Rachel. She's a cop and we need her to make sure I don't get convicted of Barb's murder. You can't bring your clown to jail with you."

My chest heaved as I locked eyes with Rachel, knowing she wasn't there, only Giggles was. Wally was an asshole, but he didn't deserve to die, but neither did Rachel or anyone I knew for that matter. Everyone who deserved it, already got it. Naming Wally bought me time and he was a believable mark. Giggles was ready to kill Rachel now and I was out of ideas.

Rachel wrapped her arms around me and squeezed me in an awkward hug. "Oh Caz, you're really in this with me, aren't you?"

"I am. I promise. Caz and Giggles, blood brothers and father and son forever."

* * *

After watching TV for hours with Rachel, or I should say Giggles, I was finally allowed to go to bed. He was staying in her body until it was time for us to kill Wally. His no-body-hopping didn't go into effect until I spilled Wally's blood.

I curled up under my covers in the fetal position, my phone pressed to my ear. I never felt so small. I dialed Barb. "Barb's phone, leave a message. I'll get back to you if I feel like it."

"Barb," I said in a whisper, so Giggles couldn't hear me. "Oh Barb, I'm so so so sorry. I didn't know. Please forgive me. You know I would never hurt you. I love you, just as much as I love Mason and Lucy. That's why it happened, because I love you. Oh, please Barb, I need you. I need you right now. I'm in a horrible mess and I don't—"

"If you are satisfied with your message press—"

I deleted the message and redialed. Just hearing Barb's voice brought me comfort. Beep: "Barb, I need your help. Please, wherever you are, help me."

CHAPTER EIGHT

Inner Clown

I wiped the remainder of the shaving cream off my face. Looking into my blue eyes, I willed myself to hold strong. Giggles had made himself comfortable in Rachel's body all week, only leaving me alone when he was forced to play cop during the day. I was biding my time, racking my brain, trying to think of a way out of killing Wally that wouldn't end with Mason, Lucy, and Rachel getting slaughtered by my own hands. I came up with nothing and Giggles was getting antsy for blood. I felt like every few minutes he would find a new way to bring up Wally. Today, we'd be seeing him at Barb's funeral, and I knew the pressure would be on.

"How'd you sleep?" Rachel asked me as I emerged from my bedroom, her smile becoming more and more like the clown puppet that sat on the couch next to her.

"Good," I lied. I hadn't slept well since I found out I killed Barb and expected I never would. My nightmare of me hurting Barb was real. Barb being scared of me was real. Those images plagued my dreams like flash photography. If it weren't for Barb's voicemail, I don't think I'd ever drift off. "How about you, how'd you sleep?"

"Great," Giggles said through Rachel. "I'm hungry, what's for breakfast?" She hopped to her feet and went to the fridge.

I followed her into the kitchen. Taking three oranges out of the fruit bowl, I juggled them. I tried not to juggle in front of Giggles. It made him excited—too excited, but it was either juggle or smoke. And smoking always made me want to drink.

Rachel threw me a fourth orange. Then a fifth. "Wow, you're so good at that. I was always horrible," she told me, her eyes following the clockwise motion of the oranges.

"As my father always said, practice makes perfect."

"My father always said practice before breakfast or you'll get the fist, but it never helped."

I stopped juggling, holding the oranges out to Rachel. "Fear may seem like a great motivating factor, but it's not. Just practice. It will come. I didn't always juggle well."

Rachel smiled a kind smile at me, taking the oranges from my hands before her smile twisted. "Fear is the *only* motivating factor."

* * *

I glanced down at Barb's still face. Her piercings were all changed to white. She looked like a snow-covered reptile queen. Her white face and her white dress were almost the same shade. She was hauntingly beautiful.

The first sob broke free against my will and from there I couldn't stop myself. I collapsed on her casket, begging for her to come back. It didn't matter that there was a crowd, I didn't care. It was about me and about Barb and that was about it.

I grew up thinking men shouldn't cry. Thinking I was a man, even when I was a boy, I never shed a tear. When the screams of children turned into sobs at the birthday party that saw the end of my father, the great Greg Giggles the clown, I didn't cry. When Lucy left me, I didn't cry. When I found Barb dead, I didn't cry. When I learned my body was used to killed Barb, I didn't cry. I held firm to the principle instilled in me by my father, by society, by my tough neighborhood—boys don't cry.

But everyone knows that's a bunch of bullshit; grown men cry all the time. The real reason I never did came down to choice. I wanted to be a good clown. No matter what you're feeling inside, a good clown always projects a smile, leaving no room for tears.

But seeing Barb in her casket affected me like nothing ever had before. I had seen my father in his casket and had attended other funerals over the years, but nothing could have prepared me for seeing Barb's dead body out on display. This was really happening. Barb was dead and being buried six feet in the ground and it was all because of me.

I felt this horrible, heavy, soul crushing guilt, like I was Atlas carrying the world on my back. It didn't matter that I wasn't in control when Giggles killed Barb. It was still my hands, still my face she saw before he pierced her eyes shut. It was still my fault. I brought Giggles home. I killed her.

Giggles was wrong about me; I didn't have it in me. I wasn't a killer. It's true, I had killed once before and didn't lose a wink of sleep. Instead of moping in guilt, I took Barb out for an impromptu celebration, telling her we were celebrating yet another hallmark in my sobriety. We ordered a shit ton of food we could never eat and had a blast. But that was different. I had killed with purpose. They deserved it. After Barb, I didn't think I could do it again, even with purpose. I couldn't carry any more weight. Barb's murder changed me.

It was Bobby V who finally peeled me from Barb, taking me outside of the church for some fresh air. He pulled a joint from his suit pocket where his pocket square should've been. He lit it and handed it to me. "Take it Caz, none of your straight edge shit. Barbie would be pissed to Hell to see you like this because of her."

"Because of her? It's because of me—it's all because of me," I wept, my face wet with tears.

"Take it," Bobby V said, shoving the joint in my mouth.

It had been a decade since I smoked a joint. I never liked the feeling that came with it. This weird half-in, half-out state of mind. I took a drag to appease him and handed it back.

"You got this Caz."

I wiped my tears on the sleeve of my suit jacket, doing all I could do to suppress new tears. I noticed Bobby V wasn't drunk. Bobby V was *always* drunk. He had given me my first beer unbeknownst to my father who had a strict no drinking rule. After running into my mother, I knew why.

"Bobby, you're sober!"

He leaned against the side of the church, shifting his weight to one leg. "Sure am. Barbie always wanted me off the bottle. It's for her, for my little Barbie. What did she want for you Caz?"

"She wanted me to be happy," I told him, swallowing the lump in my throat. "She said I always pissed on my own rainbow."

"There you have it. To honor my Barbie, you have to make yourself happy. Next time I see you, I want to see you skipping around with forest critters singing behind you."

Bobby V wasn't drunk, but I was pretty sure he was as high as a freaking kite. I pawed at my fresh tears. "I'll try," I said.

He grabbed me by my shirt collar, almost dropping his joint. "Barbie didn't do trying. She just did doing. You're gonna be happy Caz, for Barbie." He shook me. I wavered like a leaf in the wind in his bear-like mitts. His tone was rough but there was tenderness in it. "You hear me Casey Graves?!"

I needed that. I needed some literal tough love—for someone to shake me to my senses. "For Barbie," I said. "I promise."

Bobby V released me, falling into a somber mood. "That's right, for Barbie," he said, taking a drag of his joint.

* * *

There was a small group of us that went to the cemetery to see Barb off, amongst them, my family with Wally. As we walked back toward the cars, Wally slowed up to talk to me privately.

"I know we've never seen eye to eye," Wally said, stating the obvious.

I internally groaned. The last thing I needed right now was Wally's pity. Rachel, Giggles that is, was watching. Rachel was walking off to the side, keeping her distance, playing the part of a cop but I knew Giggles's eyes were locked on me. They had been since we parted ways at the church, and I went to the front to be with Bobby V, and Rachel went to the back with non-family members.

"If you need someone to talk to, I'd be more than willing to listen free of charge," Wally offered. "If you don't feel comfortable talking with me, I can suggest a colleague."

"I'm fine Wally. Thanks for the offer."

His face contorted as if to say I didn't seem fine. You didn't have to be a head shrink to know I was far from it. I was forced to look at myself this morning. I had no choice. I had to shave. Barb hated it when I looked like what she called scruffy. I wouldn't dare go to her funeral with stubble. A close shave didn't help. I had dark circles under my eyes like I had been punched in both eyes. I looked like shit, worse than that, I looked like fucking shit.

I quickened my pace to catch up with Lucy and Mason. My one-on-one time with Wally was over. Mason took my hand and asked, "Dad, did Giggles kill Aunt Barb? Mom said no, but I need to know the truth."

I picked him up, straddling him on my side. He was getting big and soon he wouldn't let me pick him up like that but for today I needed him to be a kid who needed his father. "Hey, you don't have to worry about Giggles Gimp-legs. He's not going to hurt anyone. Not Mommy, not you, no one."

"Giggles Gimp-legs?" Lucy asked.

"Yeah, that's Giggles last name."

"How do you know that?" Wally asked with an edge to his tone.

I shrugged. "I don't know. It must've been on the adoption certificate I got from the antique shop."

* * *

I held a repast for Barb at PF Changs in Atlantic City. It was her favorite restaurant. She loved the fried green beans. There was a big turnout that would have made Barb happy.

By the time I got back to my apartment, it was late. I walked in expecting to see Rachel sitting on my couch but was surprised to find Wally. He stood up as I entered.

"Uh, hey Wally," I said, looking around. "Is Rachel here?"

"Rachel?"

"Dr. Moore," I clarified.

His eyebrows hit his hairline. "Oh, you and Dr. Moore, I didn't see that."

Okay, I got my answer. Luckily for him, Rachel wasn't in the apartment. I had to get him out of there before she showed up and wanted to throw some blood on the walls. I glanced at my watch, that should be at any minute. "Wally, I don't know how you got in here, but this isn't a good time."

"I used Mason's key."

"That's for Mason. Next time, just call." I stalked into my living room, tugging on his arm like he was a child. "I want you gone. Come on, leave. You have to go, like now, like right now!"

Wally planted his feet. If I had to carry him out, I would. It may break my back, Wally was nearly two of me, but I would do it, to save his life.

I was just about to wrap my arms around him and attempt a

deadlift when he picked Giggles up from the couch. "Don't touch him!"

He quirked an eyebrow. "Why not?"

"Please tell me you didn't play with him!"

Wally cleared his throat like I offended him. "I'm an adult. I don't play with toys."

"Yeah, I had said the same thing and here I am."

His eyes cut to slits, his pupils like pinpoints. There was something in his look that let me know that asshole played with the clown. "YOU NEED TO LEAVE!"

"I believe you," he told me.

"What?!"

"I believe you that Giggles killed Barb."

I blinked rapidly, my eyelashes dusting my cheeks. "You do?" I asked.

"I treated a man years back when I was in residency. He said a clown named Giggles Gimp-legs killed his family. My colleagues all thought that he was nuts. But Peter McDermit had no history of mental illness nor did his family. When he talked about Giggles, he was so passionate about it, like you were that day Barb was found dead.

"Eventually Peter McDermit said he made everything up to cope with the death of his family and was released. But I knew he still believed the clown killed his family. I could see it in his eyes. Since that case, I hated clowns. Of course, there's no rational explanation on how a toy clown could kill people, so I thought it had to be a figment of his imagination, even if he believed it. But then today you said the name of the same clown Peter McDermit swore killed his family." He shook out his shoulders. "I don't know, I just came here to make sure you didn't drag Lucy and Mason into your shit."

"It's your shit now too Wally. You played with the clown,

didn't you?"

He glanced at it.

"That's how he does it. If you play with him, he can jump into your body. Once inside, he goes on a killing spree."

"That's absurd."

"Is it?" I asked, my heart thudding away. "Barb's dead."

"What are you saying?" Wally asked, his expressive eyebrows dancing around his forehead.

"I killed Barb."

"What?!" he gasped.

"Giggles made me kill her. He jumped inside my body, and he fucking killed her."

"I thought something screwy was going on when you made that scene at the church," he said, pulling a gun from the dress jacket he still wore from Barb's funeral. He pointed it at my chest. "I can't let what happened to Peter McDermit's family happen to mine. I'm sorry Caz."

In surrender, I put my hands in the air. "Easy Wally. Killing me won't solve anything. Giggles can jump into Mason and Rachel and now you. Giggles likes me, we have a clown connection. He's willing to spare Mason and Lucy. If you kill me, he will kill them to hurt you. Please trust me. If I thought dying would keep them safe, I'd be in that casket today with Barb. You know I'm a fuck up, but you also know how much I love Mason and Lucy."

Wally's hand shook under the weight of his gun. He didn't want to kill me any more than I wanted to kill him. "What do you propose?" he asked.

"He wants me to kill you."

Wally's eyebrows were in his hairline again. "Me? He wants you to kill me?" he asked.

"Yeah. He said he'd go silent after I did it."

"And you want me to lay down and die, is that it?"

I gave a half-hearted shrug. "It would protect Mason and Lucy."

Wally steadied his arm. "I think I'll take my chances and kill you instead," he said.

"You're smart Wally, maybe together we can outsmart him. Giggles is possessing Rachel right now. He's been in her since the night Barb was murdered. If we could find a way to— "

Chopsticks played on the door before it was pushed open. Wally's gun shifted to Rachel.

"Hurry Giggles, he knows you're in Rachel and plans on killing her!" I shouted.

Rachel collapsed to the ground as Wally jerked back dropping his gun. I picked it up.

"Thanks, Clapping Casey," Wally said. "That was a close one."

I smiled. I had just meant to buy Wally more time, but Giggles showed all his cards. I read Wally's face just as easily as if I was reading a page out of a book. Giggles was terrified. Wally's eyes, his panting breath, the sweat dripping down his temples, all betrayed him. I knew now that if his host got killed while he was inside them that meant he died too. He really was an awful clown. A good clown keeps smiling whether it's painted on their face or not. "Hold the applause Giggles," I said, shooting Wally in the face.

Wally fell back. His blood splattered all over the wall and all over me. It poured down like crimson rain, showering me in red. "Sorry Wally, I did it to protect our family. I know you would've done the same."

Rachel was by my side. "Is Giggles dead?" she asked.

"He's dead and so is Wally. It's over."

Ding, ding. Wally: two, Caz: three. And the winner is Caz.

CHAPTER NINE
Last Laugh

Six months had passed since I killed Wally and Giggles and every day my victory felt a little more like a loss. Despite that I was cleared of two murder charges, somehow Giggles got the last laugh. Peter McDermit had told me he didn't laugh and that's how I ended up. I didn't laugh. Giggles, in the end, got what he wanted. I was alone. So utterly alone without Barb. Not only had he taken my best friend, but he also took from me the one person who loved me no matter how much I screwed things up.

I had killed Wally to protect Mason and Lucy, and it had cost me the very thing I was protecting. Mason couldn't understand why I killed Wally. How could he? I killed his awesome second dad. Who was I kidding, his first dad. Mason had spent more time with Wally than me. It was Wally who saw him off to school every morning and it was Wally who tucked him in at night. It's just like Wally said, I was *Dad* one weekend a month. Yep, I killed my son's favorite dad.

Mason hadn't spoken to me since Barb's funeral. I still called him. He never answered. I texted. He never answered those either. At least Lucy answered when I called. I stuck to asking questions about Mason. She was kind, but guarded like she didn't know me anymore, or maybe it was that she didn't trust me. But there was something between us that wasn't there before, and it wasn't Wally Steinbach. Well, at least not in a literal sense. Maybe she couldn't understand why I killed Wally either.

Mason and Lucy could hate me as long as they were alive. I'd be their villain over and over again and die with a smile on my face knowing that I saved my family.

I had promised Bobby V to be happy for Barb as a way to honor her memory. I was trying. Happy my family was alive was something, even if I was freaking miserable. I suppose I broke my promise to Bobby V, but I had broken a lot of promises in the last six months: to Peter McDermit, to Giggles, to Barb. But today, I was keeping a promise to myself. I was going to piss on Giggles and watch him burn and then dance in his ashes like a psychopath.

Thanks to Rachel, all charges against me were dropped in record time, and Giggles, having been released from evidence, was returned to me. I placed him on Wally's grave. I did my best to keep my urine strictly on the clown puppet that ruined my life. Seeing that little shit's grin drenched in my urine made me feel a lot better.

Rachel and I both admitted the sex was great, but Giggles destroyed any chance of something more between us. We'd always be friends though. In a week, we'd lived through some pretty heavy trauma, and it left a mark on the both of us. Like me, Rachel got back the time Giggles stole from her, and it messed with her head. Being controlled by someone else, particularly a killer clown, is by far the scariest thing that's ever happened to me and I'm sure it was the same for her. Talk about not having control of your life.

I couldn't make her nightmares go away; however, there was one mark I could expunge for Rachel. I changed her 'Killer' tattoo into a flower.

When my case officially closed, Rachel put in for a transfer. I couldn't blame her. Her father's murder had been avenged and she was going to try to start over somewhere new. Maybe that's why

I was at Wally's grave. Maybe it was time for me to bury Giggles and move on.

I struck a match. The flame wavered in the winter air. Shielding it with my other hand, I brought the match to Giggles's fiery red hair, letting the flame latch on to his most flammable part. The orange glow danced from the matchstick to his hair. He didn't burst into flames. The fire worked slowly, taking its time to consume. I watched as his clown face melted under the heat, hoping Giggles could feel the burn in Hell.

I heard footsteps behind me. I turned to see Lucy. "I'm surprised to see you here," I said, standing in front of the smoldering clown in a failed attempt to hide what I was up to. If she couldn't see it, she could definitely smell the smoke and what reminded me of burning plastic and pine.

I hadn't seen Lucy since Wally's funeral and that was from a distance out of respect for the Steinbach family. Understandably, no one wanted me there, but I felt like I needed to be there. In the end, Wally wasn't a bad guy. He had come to my apartment that night to protect Mason and Lucy, and he gave his life for them. He deserved my respect. That's why I decided to have my clown pyre at Wally's grave. I wanted him to bear witness to Giggles burning and share in the glory with me. Giggles had started Wally's dislike of clowns and had, through me, claimed his life. It felt right to burn Giggles here, I just hoped Lucy felt the same.

Lucy brushed her dark waves off her shoulders. She was growing her hair out, it looked nice. "I come here every day," she told me in a solemn voice.

I nodded. Of course she did, Wally was her fiancé. She loved him like Mason did.

"I know I gave Wally a hard time, but he was a good guy. I'm sorry for the pain I caused you and Mason."

I hadn't apologized to Lucy about Wally or talked about what happened with her. Rachel had done the explaining for me as a friend, as a cop, and someone who had been there. I feared Lucy thought I killed Wally in some warped way to get her back. You know, removed my competition. That, and I couldn't bear knowing for a fact she hated me. The cold shoulder from Mason had me on the edge of a shot glass. Lucy's hatred would send me headfirst into the bottle.

"What about him?" Lucy said, pointing at Giggles. "Are you sorry for killing him?"

I craned my neck to glance at Giggles behind me. His lips dripped off his face like he was made of wax, his once creepy smile now a lopsided frown. "You believe me about the clown?"

"I do."

I took a deep breath in and exhaled through my nose, piping hot air into the cold. That was refreshing to know. If she believed me about the clown, that meant she believed I killed Wally to save her and Mason. "I'd be lying if I said a part of me didn't feel bad for Giggles," I admitted, shoving my hands in my coat pockets. "He had a shit dad, way worse than I am and nothing like my father. If he'd grown up with my dad, he would have become a clown like he always wanted. And if not, my father would've still been proud of him. I've learned good fathers aren't born they're made. My father wasn't perfect, but he tried his hardest, and that's what I'm going to do. I'm gonna prove to Mason I can be a good father like Wally was."

A series of pops came from the fire, directing our attention to it. Together, we watched Giggles's frown sizzle in the fire.

"Mason's been talking about you."

My eyes met hers in a clash of sky blue. "He has?" I asked, my hope finding its way into my voice.

"He's coming around. I know he misses you. He's still

drawing dinosaurs but now he's drawing them juggling."

I smiled. "Now that's something, a dinoclown."

"He's practicing juggling again."

My heart beat proudly in my chest. My boy juggling. I could feel the tears as they fought to come free. I swallowed them. "That's, that's so awesome."

"I wasn't supposed to tell you that, so it's between us," Lucy said with a wink. "He's worried you're going to think he's not very good and wants to wait to see you until he has it perfect. He really wants to surprise you."

"My father always said practice makes perfect, but he doesn't have to wait to see me," I said. "I don't want Mason to think he has to be perfect for me."

"Practice makes perfect," Lucy repeated as if she was mulling it over. "My father always said to my older brother 'Practice before breakfast or you'll get the fist.' My brother wanted to be perfect and couldn't be. I don't want that for Mason. You're right, I'm not gonna let him wait until he's perfect to show you."

My face twisted under the burden of my thoughts. "Practice before breakfast or you'll get the fist . . . Your abusive father . . . Lucy, was Marcus Gable your brother?"

Tears streamed down her face, but she remained composed. "My father was so cruel to him. The only thing worse than the physical abuse was the mental abuse. It left my brother unable to do anything. Do you remember the clown tattoo that I used to have on my shoulder, the tat I removed for Wally?"

"Of course." I could never forget it. That clown tattoo was my sign from the higher powers that Lucy was the one for me.

"I had it tattooed for Marcus," she told me as she wiped tears. "For my brother who died. It was his face with clown paint. I had no picture of him and was beginning to forget what he looked like. I was so young when he died. I don't even know if my tattoo was a good representation, but it was how I saw him with my little girl eyes. Even though I had the tattoo removed, I kept a picture of it so I would always remember him." She shook her head at herself. "I didn't realize Giggles was the clown my father had bought for my brother until you called him Gimp-legs. I never forgot my father calling him that."

Oh wow, in a way Giggles had brought Lucy and me together. It was his face on her shoulder. The thought of it made me lightheaded.

Lucy held me in the frame of her thick, black lashes. Her tears were gone, but her eyes remained glassy as if a layer of ice had frozen over them. She had never looked so beautiful. "I never told you about Marcus because I couldn't talk about him. About what happened to him, but I should've. So, you could have understood. When you hit me, I left because at that moment I thought of my brother and was so full of hate and rage that I thought I could kill you, really kill you, and it scared me. I didn't want to hurt you."

"If I ever laid a hand on you again, I would want you to kill me."

She shook her head at me, her breathing becoming erratic. "You don't understand what I'm telling you Caz. Giggles isn't the only killer in the family."

My heart pumped faster; the sound echoed between my eardrums. Did she know what I had done?

"When I was about Mason's age, I started a fire that killed Marcus. I was trying to kill my father, but he managed to get out of the house with only a few burns and poor Marcus, he got trapped in the fire because of his wheelchair and died. I never meant to hurt him. I loved Marcus. He was my big brother."

I wanted to take her hand but resisted. I didn't want to push her further away from me. "It's okay. You meant well," I told her.

She did, in a really messed up, misguided way. Look at the family she came from, you couldn't blame her; she was just a little kid. "You were trying to protect your brother," I said. "That makes you brave. You didn't know any better."

"Maybe not then, but I did when I started the fire that killed your mother."

That took the air right out of my lungs.

"I hated her for not being there for you after your father died. She should've been there," Lucy said, the muscle in her jaw jumping. "I killed her because that's how much I love you Caz. It's just like how you killed Wally to protect Mason and me. Mason doesn't understand but I do."

The corner of my lips turned up, my smile shifting into a sideways grin as a hiccup of a laugh escaped my lips. A feeling of belonging washed over me, sending a shiver of pins and needles down my spine to my gloved fingertips. It was the feeling you get when you step over the threshold of your home after a long vacation to see your faithful dog waiting for you with doggy kisses.

My hand went to my mouth to smother a hysterical titter that broke free.

"What's so funny? I'm serious Caz. I need you to know the truth. I can't hold it in any longer." Her frustration brought her to tears.

I suppressed another laugh, letting it sit in my throat. I took Lucy's hand and kissed the top of it. "Lucy, you and I are a perfect match. You killed my mother for me, and I killed your father for you."

Her tears stopped abruptly as if by magic. "You did?" she asked, her eyes wide with what I knew was disbelief.

"I'd been sober for about three months at that point and you'd just turned me away for what felt like the hundredth time. I couldn't turn to the bottle, so I turned to your father. I found the son of a bitch living in a shelter in New York City. I deliberately ran into him in an alley. He was looking to get his next score, and I sold him a bad batch. I waited for him to die and took the evidence."

"You never told me."

"I wasn't sure how you'd take it."

She smiled a toothy grin, and a giggle of laughter was shared between us.

"I would have sent you a thank you card," she said, still laughing.

A gust of wind whipped through the cemetery. I held our hands overhead and spun Lucy around so we could dance in Giggles ashes. It felt good to keep a promise. "How about you skip the card and let me take you out to dinner instead? First date and all of that. Start fresh. New us."

"A second chance," she said.

My heart thumped away in my chest. "A second chance at happiness. What do you say Lucy?"

"Let's try," she said as a smile teased at the corners of her lips. "Wally and Barb would want it that way."

"Barb yes, she would've wanted this. Wally, I don't think so, but it's nice to know I get the last laugh after all."

My lips met Lucy's, and I was able to keep another promise that day. I was happy. So happy that my heart clapped for joy.

The End . . .

THANKS FOR READING!

If this book helped you escape, if only for a moment, please consider taking the time to leave a review or star rating on Amazon or whatever platform you use. It would warm the cockles of my little, black heart to hear from you.

Looking for something else to read? Don't forget to check out my other books on Amazon.

Follow me on social media (I'm on all platforms under Holly Knightley). Sign up for my newsletter for the latest news, glimpse into my wacky process, and occasional freebie. Stay spooky and happy reading!

WANT MORE?